Archibald Alexander

Outlines of Moral Science

SALZWASSER
VERLAG

Archibald Alexander

Outlines of Moral Science

Reprint of the original, first published in 1863.

1st Edition 2022 | ISBN: 978-3-37500-147-6

Verlag (Publisher): Salzwasser Verlag GmbH, Zeilweg 44, 60439 Frankfurt, Deutschland
Vertretungsberechtigt (Authorized to represent): E. Roepke, Zeilweg 44, 60439 Frankfurt, Deutschland
Druck (Print): Books on Demand GmbH, In de Tarpen 42, 22848 Norderstedt, Deutschland

MORAL SCIENCE.

OUTLINES

OF

MORAL SCIENCE.

BY

ARCHIBALD ALEXANDER, D.D.,

LATE PROFESSOR IN THE THEOLOGICAL SEMINARY AT PRINCETON, N. J.

NEW YORK:

1863.

CONTENTS.

PAGE

CHAPTER I.

CONSCIENCE, OR THE MORAL FACULTY, . . . 19

CHAPTER II.

THE MORAL FACULTY, ORIGINAL AND UNIVERSAL, . 27

CHAPTER III.

A MORAL FACULTY BEING SUPPOSED, WHETHER ITS DICTATES ARE UNIFORM, ... 30

CHAPTER IV.

HOW FAR ALL MEN ARE AGREED IN THEIR MORAL JUDGMENTS, ... 39

CHAPTER V.

WHETHER CONSCIENCE IS THE SAME AS THE UNDERSTANDING, OR A FACULTY DIFFERENT FROM AND INDEPENDENT OF IT, ... 40

CHAPTER VI.

THE MORAL SENSE COMPARED WITH TASTE, . . . 44

PAGE

CHAPTER VII.

MORAL OBLIGATION, ... 48

CHAPTER VIII.

THE SUPREMACY OF CONSCIENCE, . . . 60

CHAPTER IX.

WHETHER WE ALWAYS DO RIGHT BY OBEYING THE DICTATES OF CONSCIENCE? 64

CHAPTER X.

WHETHER THERE IS IN THE MIND A LAW OR RULE, BY WHICH MAN JUDGES OF THE MORALITY OF PARTICULAR ACTIONS? 73

CHAPTER XI.

THE MORAL FEELING WHICH ACCOMPANIES EVERY MORAL JUDGMENT, ... 78

CHAPTER XII.

BELIEF IN GOD, AS CONNECTED WITH THE OPERATION OF CONSCIENCE, ... 84

CHAPTER XIII.

MORAL AGENCY, AND WHAT IS NECESSARY TO IT, . 89

CHAPTER XIV.

MAN A MORAL AGENT, ... 97

CHAPTER XV.

MAN NOT UNDER A FATAL NECESSITY, . . . 102

PAGE

CHAPTER XVI.

MAN'S DIRECTION AND GOVERNMENT OF HIS ACTIONS, AND HIS CONSEQUENT RESPONSIBILITY, . . 107

CHAPTER XVII.

OBJECTIONS TO THE UNIFORM INFLUENCE OF MOTIVES, 117

CHAPTER XVIII.

SUMMARY VIEW OF LIBERTY, ... 125

CHAPTER XIX.

THE KIND OF INDIFFERENCE WHICH HAS BEEN CONSIDERED ESSENTIAL TO FREE AGENCY, . . 128

CHAPTER XX.

WHETHER MEN ARE ACCOUNTABLE FOR THEIR MOTIVES; OR WHETHER DESIRES AND AFFECTIONS WHICH PRECEDE VOLITION, HAVE A MORAL CHARACTER? 136

CHAPTER XXI.

THE DIVISION OF MOTIVES, INTO RATIONAL AND ANIMAL, ... 142

CHAPTER XXII.

WHETHER MORALITY BELONGS TO PRINCIPLES AS WELL AS ACTS, OR IS CONFINED TO ACTS ALONE? 147

CHAPTER XXIII.

MORAL HABITS, ... 155

PAGE

CHAPTER XXIV.

THE NATURE OF VIRTUE, ... 159

CHAPTER XXV.

THE NATURE OF VIRTUE, CONTINUED. DIFFERENT HYPOTHESES, ... 171

CHAPTER XXVI.

THE NATURE OF VIRTUE, CONTINUED, . . . 184

CHAPTER XXVII.

WHETHER VIRTUE AND VICE BELONG ONLY TO ACTIONS? 190

CHAPTER XXVIII.

THE AUTHOR OF OUR BEING CONSIDERED IN RELATION TO MORAL SCIENCE, ... 200

CHAPTER XXIX.

THE PHENOMENA OF THE UNIVERSE, . . . 207

CHAPTER XXX.

DUTIES OF MAN TO THE CREATOR AS THUS MANIFESTED, ... 215

PREFACE.

THE work now offered to the public is the last which proceeded from the lamented author's hand. In the days which immediately preceded his peaceful departure out of the present life, and while his powers were free from all clouds and weakness, he spoke of these papers as nearly prepared for the press, and consigned them with that intention to two of his sons. With a trifling exception, the whole had been carefully transcribed by the hand of filial duty from his own character, which, more from declining eyesight than any manual debility, had lost its former boldness and clearness, and had become difficult. In giving his commands respecting the printing, he empowered his representatives to use a discretion as to lesser points in the form, which has been found to be almost entirely needless.

The ministers of Christ who in this and other countries remember the instructions of Dr. Alexander, will be best able to judge of this production. They will recognise in it the doctrines and arguments which characterized the author's theological method, and will doubtless prize it as a comprehensive syllabus, even while they miss that copiousness, vivacity, and warmth, which added efficacy to his oral teachings.

The subject of Ethical Philosophy may be said to have engaged the mind of the author for at least threescore years. The earliest vestiges of his boyish studies show proofs of this, in connection with the metaphysical inquiries which afterwards became his favourite employment of mind. Though in after years he was almost daily adding to his knowledge of ethical literature, with an avidity which was unabated to the last, and which sought to be satisfied with the most recondite disquisitions in the ancient tongues no less than our own, he nevertheless appears to have arrived at definite conclusions very early, and to have maintained them with little change. It was not the habit of his mind, as is well known, to accumulate authorities, to load his discourses with learned citation, or even to break the continuity of his analytical discourse by unnecessary sallies against opponents. Amidst a life of perpetual reading, of which he held the spoils in his memory with singular exactness and tenacity, he persevered in seeking and presenting truth with the minimum of quoted aid. This quality of his thinking will be all the rather obvious in a treatise like the present, which, as an epitome of extended results, necessarily leaves out a thousand particulars of the process and all the lighter play of illustration.

During the period of nearly forty years, in which he was theological professor, the author had an exercise, for the most part weekly, in Mental and Moral Science; as a transition from college work and a recapitulation of juvenile studies. The lectures thus delivered were the basis of the succinct manual now made public. All its parts were thrown into a shape suitable for the printing, except the closing chapters on the Being and Attributes of God, and the duties resulting from the relation of the Creator and creature.

These portions not having been copied remain in autograph, and may be regarded as the last written speculations of one who employed his pen almost every day for more than half a century. If the articulation of this important member with the body of the discourse seem less obvious than might be desired, it will become sufficiently clear to such as reflect on the great earnestness with which, in the former part, the author maintains the intuitive perceptions of conscience as independent of every doctrine of theology, even the greatest.

A casual inspection will be enough to show any reader that this is a book of elements; laying down principles, clearing the statement of fundamental questions, and marking limits around the science. It does not descend therefore to the more usual and far easier work of gathering, naming, and tabling the human duties. This labour he did not undervalue; indeed it was part of his course of instructions; and his unfinished manuscripts contain large contributions towards a separate work in this kind, embracing even all the range of duties which are properly Christian and even ecclesiastical. But the treatise now presented was intended to lay foundations and elucidate principles; in other words it is upon the Philosophy of Morals. At the same time, however, that the topics here discussed are some of the most puzzling which have exercised human acuteness, patience and abstraction, from the days of the Greek authors till our own, they are such as cannot be set aside or turned over to others as matter for authority; for the very reason that they concern the springs of daily action, are presented every hour in the household, and meet us in the very babblings of the nursery. And notwithstanding the tenuity of the objects brought under review, and the delicate thread of inquiry along which the analysis must often feel its way, the writer seems to derive an advantage from his unusual simplicity and transparency of language, which might betray a superficial reader into the opinion that the train of argument is not original or profound. In none of the author's works is this quality more apparent than in that which follows.

One of the reasons which impelled Dr. Alexander, at a stage of life which was encumbered with cares and infirmities, to address himself to this toilsome composition, was the desire to furnish a Manual for the young men of America, in our colleges, theological seminaries, and other schools. He was repeatedly besought to supply such a volume, and never wavered in his persuasion that it was necessary; especially when he saw with pain to what an extent the place of a class-book was occupied by the great but dangerous work of Archdeadeacon Paley. In common with other sound ethical inquiries he recognised the valne of President Wayland's labours, and the eloquence and richness of Dr. Chalmers's striking but fragmentary contributions. Yet he thought he saw room for a brief hand-book level to the capacity of all; and he had a natural and pardonable desire common to all original thinkers, to give vent to his own opinions in his own order. In regard to the ethical system here expounded, the work may safely be left to speak for itself. It is positive and didactic rather than controversial, yet there is scarcely a chapter which, however tranquil and subdued in its tone, will not awaken opposition in some quarter or other. The polemic aspect of the treatise is, however, apparent only in cases where to avoid the naming of opponents would have been an affectation no less than a breach of trust. No one, whatever his private dissent may be, will justly complain that his opinions have been treated with unfairness or rigour. The connection of ethics with theology is such that no one can treat of the nature of virtue, of the will, of motives, and the like, without at least indicating his tendencies in regard to the great dividing questions of revelation; which only increases the necessity for giving the right direction to juvenile studies; unless we would receive to the professional curriculum minds already pre-occupied with ethical tenets subversive of great truths in law, politics and theology. Those who have watched the progress of modern speculation will not fail to apprehend the drift of this observation. Yet the way in which even these somewhat delicate parts of moral science are here set forth, is such as never to awaken suspicion of any sinister intention, or to betray any irregular passage into a neighbouring but separate science. Even those discussions which, at a first view, might seem to belong rather to natural theology, were deliberately assigned to their place after long experience in teaching, as pertaining to the limits where the two fields osculate if they do not cut, and with a clear pre-eminence given to the ethical side of the truths common to both.

The labours of the author were arrested by his last illness, when the work here published was complete indeed as has been said, but not ready for the press in the sense of being revised and corrected. It is this which has made these prefatory pages necessary; an introduction from the author's hand would have precluded all such attempts as weak and impertinent.

As he gave the work in charge with his dying lips, after having no doubt offered it to God in many of his solicitous and elevated thoughts during the preparation, so it is now humbly dedicated to Him, with ut whose blessing, no human effort, even in the best cause, is other than worthless.

NEW YORK, Aug. 1, 1852.

MORAL SCIENCE.

CHAPTER I.

CONSCIENCE, OR THE MORAL FACULTY.

As all men, when reason is developed, have a faculty by which they can discern a difference between objects of sight which are beautiful and those which are deformed, so all men possess the power of discerning a difference between actions, as to their moral quality. The judgment thus formed is immediate, and has no relation to the usefulness or injuriousness to human happiness, of the objects contemplated.

All men discern moral qualities.

Whatever difference of opinion may exist respecting the origin of this faculty, it is universally admitted that men, in all ages and countries, have judged some actions to be good and deserving of appro

True in all ages

bation, while they have judged others to be bad, and of ill desert.

In all languages, we find words expressive of the ideas of moral excellence, and moral evil.

Agreement of mankind.

In the laws and penalties established in all ages throughout the world, it is evidently implied that some actions ought to be done, and others avoided. In cases of flagrant injustice or ingratitude, all men, of every country and of every age, agree in their judgment of their moral evil. There is, in regard to such actions, no more difference in the judgment of men, than respecting the colour of grass, or the taste of honey. If any man does not perceive grass to be green, or honey to be sweet, we do not thence conclude that men's bodily senses are not similarly constituted, but that the organs of the individual who does not see and taste as other men do, are defective, or depraved by disease.

Case proposed must be simple.

To determine whether all men have one original moral faculty, the case proposed for their moral judgment should be simply good or evil. For a complex act, in which there is something good and something evil, or rather where there must be an accurate weighing of motives in order to ascertain he quality of the action, is not a proper test as to the existence of a uniformity of moral judgment in men. Therefore, the historical fact adduced by Dr. Paley,* from the history of Valerius Maximus, is not at all suited to his purpose; because the case is very complex, and one on which it is difficult to determine at first view, what the true moral character of the action is. The facts, as related by him, are as follows: The father of Caius Toranius had been proscribed by the Triumvirate. Caius Toranius—coming over to the interests of that party—discovered his father's place of concealment to the officers who were in pursuit of him, and gave them, withal, a description of his person by which they might distinguish him. The old man, more anxious for the safety and fortunes of his son than for the little that might remain of his own life, began

Case of Toranius irrelative.

* In the chapter of his Moral Philosophy, under the head "The Moral Sense."

immediately to inquire of the officers whether his son were well, and whether he had done his duty to the satisfaction of the generals. 'That son (replied one of the officers), so dear to thy affections, has betrayed thee to us; by his information thou art apprehended, and diest.' With this, the officer struck a poniard to his heart, and the unhappy parent fell, affected not so much by his fate, as by the means to which he owed it." Now, the question is, if this story were related to the wild boy caught some years ago in the woods of Hanover, or to a savage without experience and without instruction, cut off in his infancy from all intercourse with his species, and consequently under no possible influence of example, authority, education, sympathy, or habit, whether or not such a one would feel upon the relation any degree of that sentiment of disapprobation of Toranius's conduct which w feel.

Why it affords no criterion.

In our judgment, such a case would afford no criterion by which to determine whether men possess constitutionally a *moral sense*. For, in the first place, the trial would be no better than if the question were proposed to a child two years old, in whose mind the moral faculty is not yet developed A human being, arrived at adult age without instruction or communication with others, would be —as it relates to the mind—in a state differing very little from that of infancy. It is not held that the moral sense will be exercised without the usual means by which human faculties are developed. If an organical defect in the brain should prevent the intellectual faculties from coming into exercise, the unhappy individual thus deprived of reason would prove nothing in regard to the operations of reason where it is developed. So, also, if a human being were brought up from early infancy in a dark dungeon, and if no information were communicated to him, the mental faculties would not be developed, and it would be absurd to have recourse to such a one to ascertain what faculties belong to the human mind. The same remark will apply to the case of the wild boy, referred to by Dr. Paley; and also, though in an inferior degree, to savages of the most degraded class.

Let it then be fairly understood what it is which is asserted in regard to conscience, as an original, universal faculty. It is that every human mind, when its faculties have been developed, and have arrived at some degree of maturity, discerns a quality in certain actions which is termed moral; that is, it intuitively perceives that some actions are right and some wrong.

What is meant by an original, universal faculty.

Another objection to the historical fact adduced by Dr. Paley, is, that it presents to the mind, not a case of simple, unmixed good or evil, but a complex case, in which—before a judgment can be formed of the action of the son—it must be decided whether a man ought to be governed by a regard to the welfare of a parent, or to the public good. If the son believed that the party in pursuit of his father was promoting the public good, he might feel that he ought to be governed by this rather than by filial affection. Here, then, we have presented a complex and difficult case in morals, about which men would be very apt to

Paley's instance complex.

differ; and we are to determine whether all men—even those totally uneducated—would view it in the same light.

To render the case a suitable one to be a test of the question under consideration, it should be supposed that the father was acting in conformity with the strictest principles of rectitude; that his life was sought by wicked men, aiming not at the good of the commonwealth but its destruction; and that the son, in betraying the place of his concealment, was actuated by mercenary motives, or by unjust and unnatural dislike to a good parent. If a case like this were presented to a thousand persons, from as many different parts of the world, there would be but one judgment and one feeling, all would judge the conduct of the son to be blamable. Different degrees of moral disapprobation would be felt by those whose moral faculty was in a cultivated state; but there would be no difference in the opinion entertained of his conduct. All would feel disapprobation, accompanied by a desire for the punishment of the

A proper case supposed.

offender. It is found that savages appear to have but an obscure exercise of conscience, but in proportion as their minds are cultivated, this faculty becomes more manifest, and operates mor forcibly.

CHAPTER II.

THE MORAL FACULTY, ORIGINAL AND UNIVERSAL.

If conscience were not an original faculty, enabling us to form a conception of moral qualities, man could never acquire such an idea by any other means. The opinion, therefore, that moral feelings are merely the effect of instruction and education, is erroneous. For every class of simple ideas there must be an appropriate faculty, without which these ideas can never be acquired. In regard to the bodily senses, this is too evident to be called in question. Without the organ of vision the simple idea of light and colours could never b communicated by any instructions; without the organ of hearing, no idea of sound can be conveyed; and so of the other senses. And it is equally true of that knowledge which is acquired by

Moral ideas otherwise unattainable.

what some have called the internal senses If there were in man no such faculty as taste, by which beauty is perceived, no idea of the beautiful could possibly be communicated. A horse has no perception of the beauty of a scene which perhaps enchants his rider, even though the animal sees all the objects with equal distinctness. So it is in regard to moral qualities. There must be an original faculty to give us the simple idea which we have of morality; otherwise the idea of virtue or vice could never have entered the human mind, and the feelings of moral obligation, of which all men are conscious, would never have been felt.

The utilitarian objection.

I am aware that those who advocate the utilitarian scheme, resolve all our ideas of morality and moral obligation into the mere principles of benefit or injury, apprehended to be connected with each action. Dr. Paley informs us, that the subject continued to be involved in impenetrable mystery, until he took this view of it.

It is deemed useless to argue this point; it cannot be decided by reasoning. The appeal must be made to the consciousness of every man.

Appeal to consciousness.

If any one persists in declaring that he sees no evil in any action but as it is evidently detrimental to human happiness, nothing can be said in the way of argument to alter convictions derived from his own consciousness. All that is proper to be said is, that the mind of such a person is differently constituted from that of most men; or rather that an impartial examination of this subject has not been made. It is recommended to such persons carefully to scrutinize the exercises of their own minds; they will perceive that the idea of virtue or moral good is entirely distinct from that of mere utility. There is, indeed, a connection between these two things which is very intimate, and this seems to have misled many in their judgments. Virtuous conduct leads to happiness, and is always beneficial; yet our idea of its moral character is not derived from this consideration, but from the nature of the action itself.

CHAPTER III.

A MORAL FACULTY BEING SUPPOSED, WHETHER ITS DICTATES ARE UNIFORM?

ONE of the strongest objections which has been brought against the doctrine laid down is, that among men of different countries, and of entirely different education, there is no agreement in their judgments respecting the morality or immorality of the same actions. Whereas, it is alleged, that if such a faculty were originally a part of man's constitution, there would as certainly be uniformity, as in the perception of objects by the external senses. Now, if the dictates of conscience in men of different ages and countries do so much differ, does it not show that the moral feelings of men are just what education makes them? And what is gained by maintaining the existence

Objection from alleged disagreement.

of a moral faculty, as part of man's original constitution?

It will, I think, be admitted, that in all countries and conditions in which men have been found, there exists a perception of a difference in the moral character of actions; that is, some things are accounted wrong, which ought not to be done, and some right, which ought to be done.

Moral differences perceived by all.

Again, it has never been pretended as being a matter of fact, that between men of different countries there is a total difference in the opinions entertained respecting what is right and what is wrong. A few cases only of difference are alleged, in which this discrepance is observed; but in regard to those actions which are reckoned good or evil, there is a general agreement. As to those in which there seems to be a fundamental difference, an explanation will be given hereafter. No nation, or tribe, or class of mankind has ever held that it is a virtuous and proper thing to do injury to men, or that there is no more harm in taking away life than in preserving it. It

Total disagreement not pretended.

has never been held that ingratitude—though everywhere common in practice—is a commendable thing; or that deceit and fraud are as praiseworthy as honesty and fair dealing.

Proof from common estimate of character.

There is in every country a difference made in the estimation of the character of men, derived from the course of their conduct. Some men are reckoned good in the public estimation, while others are considered wicked; the former obtain esteem, the latter are despised. That course of conduct which secures a good reputation, does not in any country consist of actions which we consider wicked, but of actions which in all countries are considered praiseworthy; and men have never obtained a bad character by a course of good behaviour.

Practice does not prove absence of moral judgment.

It is also important to observe, that the conduct of a people is not a fair test of the internal state of the mind, as it relates to morals. We know that individuals often pursue a course of conduct, which in their serious moments they condemn. Yet the power of temptation, and the habit of indulgence are such, that notwithstanding the convictions of conscience, they continue in a course of evil-doing. It would be a very inconclusive inference to determine from their habitual conduct, that they acted in accordance with the dictates of conscience. And what is true of individuals, may be true of nations and tribes. Those customs which they have received from their forefathers, may not meet with the approbation of their moral sense, and yet such is the force of an established custom, that they go on in the way in which they were brought up.

Error is in the application.

But a more satisfactory explanation of those facts, in which men seem conscientiously to go contrary to the fundamental principles of morals, is, that the principle on which they act is correct, but through ignorance or error they make an erroneous application of it.

Infanticide

When parents murder their own female children—a thing very customary in China—it is on the principle that they will be subject to more misery than happiness in the world; and therefore it is doing them a favour. Here, the general principle is correct—that parents should consult the best interests of their offspring—but the mistake is in the application. The same may be said of the practice of exposing aged parents, when they become incapable of enjoying the world.

Heathen enormities.

As to those acts of cruelty which the Pagans perform in their religious services, (the wife committing herself to the flames with the body of her deceased husband; children voluntarily thrown into the Ganges, or persons devoting their own lives by falling under the car of Juggernaut,) they are performed on the principle that what God requires, or what pleases him, or what will secure happiness for ourselves or friends, should be done. It is true that the will of God should be obeyed, whatever sacrifice he may require; their error is in thinking that such sacrifices are required by Him.

CHAPTER IV.

HOW FAR ALL MEN ARE AGREED IN THEIR MORAL JUDGMENTS.

As the subject of morals is very extensive, and particular cases may be complicated, and as men are not only ignorant, but prejudiced by the errors received in their education, it is no more wonderful that they should adopt different opinions on these subjects than on other matters. That, however, which is true in regard to every department of human knowledge, is doubtless true in regard to the science of morals. There are certain self-evident truths, which are intuitively perceived by every one who has the exercise of reason, as soon as they are presented to the mind. In regard to these fundamental truths, there has never been any difference of opinion.

First Truths in Morals.

It is not meant that all men distinctly think of these primary truths in morals; for many are so inattentive, or so much occupied with sensible objects, that they can scarcely be said ever to reflect on the subject of moral duty. But let an act of manifest injustice be performed before their eyes, and among a thousand spectators there will be but one opinion, and but one feeling. If a strong man, for example, violently takes away the property of one weaker than himself, and for no other reason than because he covets it, all men will condemn the act. So, if any one who has received from another great benefits, not only refuses to make any grateful return, but on the contrary, returns evil for good, all men will agree in judging his conduct to be wrong. All intuitively discern that for a ruler to punish the innocent and spare the guilty, is morally wrong. It is not true, in fact, that there is no agreement among men as to the fundamental principles of morals. Their judgments on these points are as uniform as on the axioms of mathematics; as in their agreement that the starry firmament is grand and beautiful; yea, as uniform as concerning the greenness of the grass, or the varied colours of the rainbow.

Mr. Locke, in his zeal to disprove the existence of innate truths, attempts to render uncertain some of these first truths of morals.

Locke

When we go beyond these first principles, we may expect to find men falling into grievous error respecting moral duty; and this often appears in their application of general principles to particular cases. Most men either reason not at all, or reason badly, and draw from sound principles incorrect conclusions. For the most part, they receive implicitly what they have been taught; or they are governed in their opinions by the common sentiment; or they adopt as true what is most for their interest, or most agreeable to their feelings. And as men are often under the influence of feelings or passions which produce perturbation of mind, and so bias the judgment, it is easy to see how errors of judgment respecting moral conduct, in many cases, may spring up. And yet it is true, that there are primary

Intuitive judgments.

truths in morals, in which all men agree, so soon as they are presented to the mind. As in other cases, by pursuing a course of sophistical reasonings, conclusions may be arrived at which are contradictory to these first principles, and this will produce perplexity; or even a kind of speculative assent may be yielded to such conclusions of ratiocination; but whenever it is necessary to form a practical judgment, the belief of intuitive truths must prevail. Our assent in these cases is not a matter of choice, but of necessity.

Berkeley.

Bishop Berkeley thought he had demonstrated that there was no external world; and many others thought there was no flaw in his reasoning: but all these speculative skeptics were, nevertheless, practical believers in the real existence of external objects. Atheistical and infidel philosophers have often endeavoured to prove that there is no intrinsic difference between right and wrong, and some of them probably persuaded themselves that this opinion was true; but these very men, when an act of great injustice towards themselves or friends was committed, could not but feel that it was morally evil; and when they saw an act of disinterested benevolence performed, they could not but approve it as morally good.

CHAPTER V.

WHETHER CONSCIENCE IS THE SAME AS THE UNDERSTANDING, OR A FACULTY DIFFERENT FROM AND INDEPENDENT OF IT.

SOME have maintained that our moral feelings and judgments are the exercise of a peculiar sense, and that the perceptions and feelings of this sense cannot be referred to the understanding. Such as maintain this theory suppose, also, that the dictates of conscience are infallibly correct, if the mind is in a proper state.

State of the question.

Others have maintained that the dictates of conscience are the judgments of the understanding, in regard to moral duty, and that, of course, an error in the judgment of the understanding must affect the decisions or dictates of conscience. To clear

Truths premised.

this subject, if possible, from all obscurity and perplexity, I would make the following remarks:

1st. The exercise of the moral faculty, or conscience, is not simply an intellectual act; it is complex, including two things —a judgment and an emotion, or feeling of a peculiar kind.

The act complex

2d. All judgments of the mind, whatever be the subject of them, appertain to the understanding. This comprehensive faculty includes all intellectual acts, whether relating to external objects, mathematical relations, natural beauty and sublimity, or moral duty. So far, therefore, as conscience is a judgment respecting any moral subject, so far it is an exercise of the understanding. We have not one faculty by which we discern physical truths, another by which we judge of mathematical theorems, and another for matters of taste; but all these are the one and the same understanding, exercised on different objects. Accordingly, when moral qualities are the objects of our contemplation, it is not a dif-

As judgment, it is intellectual.

ferent faculty from the reason or understanding which thinks and judges, but the same, exercised on other subjects; and the only difference is in the object. Our conclusion therefore is, that so far as conscience is an intellectual act or judgment of the mind, so far it belongs to the understanding.

More than intellectual acts in conscience.

3d. But as more is included under the name *conscience* than a mere intellectual act or judgment, and as this judgment is attended with a peculiar feeling, called moral, and easily distinguished from all other emotions; and as mere emotion or feeling can with no propriety be referred to the reason, therefore conscience is, so far as this is concerned, different from the understanding.

Harmony of mental operations as to morals.

4th. If the moral judgments of the mind were from a faculty distinct from the understanding, and often differing from it, the harmony of the mental operations would be destroyed. While reason led to one conclusion, conscience might dictate the contrary. And upon this theory, conscience must always be correct, unless the faculty be morbid.

How far conscience is of reason.

All experience and history show that men may act under the influence of an erroneous conscience. The dictates of conscience are always in conformity with the practical judgments of reason. When these are erroneous, conscience is erroneous. The conclusion therefore is that conscience is not a distinct faculty from reason, so far as it consists in a judgment of the quality of moral acts. Reason or understanding is the genus; the judgments of conscience are the species. Reason has relation to all intelligible subjects; the moral faculty is conversant about moral qualities alone.

CHAPTER VI.

THE MORAL SENSE COMPARED WITH TASTE.

The term moral sense.

FROM what was said in the preceding chapter, it appears that conscience, or the moral sense, is not a simple but a compound faculty, including both an intellectual act or judgment, and a peculiar feeling or emotion. The name moral sense was probably adopted to express this feeling, or internal emotion. It will serve perhaps to illustrate this subject, if we bring into view another faculty, between which and the moral sense there is a remarkable analogy. I refer to what is commonly called Taste, or that faculty by which men are in some degree capable of perceiving and relishing the beauties of nature and art. In this there is a judgment respecting that quality denominated Beauty, but there is also a vivid emotion of a peculiar kind, accompanying this judgment. The external objects in which beauty is resident, might be distinctly seen, and yet no such quality be perceived; as was before mentioned in regard to certain animals, whose sight and hearing is more acute than those of men, and which yet appear to be utterly insensible of the quality called beauty.

If the question should be raised whether Taste is merely an exercise of the understanding, the proper answer would be precisely as in the case of conscience, viz., so far as it consists in judgment, it appertains to the intellectual faculty; but so far as it consists in emotion, it does not. And in this, as in matters of conscience, errors of judgment will affect the emotions produced. In cultivating Taste, it is of the utmost importance that correct opinions be adopted in relation to the objects of this faculty.

Analogy between judgments of taste and of conscience.

The question may perhaps be asked, why either of these should be considered a distinct faculty of the mind. In regard to mental faculties or powers, there is a want of agreement among philosophers, as to what is requisite to entitle any mental operation to be referred to a distinct and original faculty. In these two cases, there exists in the mind a capacity for perceiving peculiar qualities in certain appropriate objects. Though the ideas of beauty and morality are judgments of the understanding, it requires a faculty suited to the objects, to enable the understanding to obtain the simple ideas of beauty and morality. We can conceive of a rational mind without such a capacity. There is also in these faculties, the susceptibility of a peculiar emotion, dissimilar from all others; and these two things constitute the faculty of Taste or Conscience But it is a matter of no importance whether taste and conscience be called distinct and original faculties, if what has been said respecting their nature be admitted.

Whether in either case a distinct faculty.

There is in the human mind a capacity of discerning what is termed beauty, in the works of nature and art. This judgment is accompanied by a pleasurable emotion, and to this capacity or

Original susceptibility in both.

susceptibility we give the name Taste. There is also a power of discerning moral qualities, which conception is also attended with a vivid emotion; and to this power or faculty we give the name Conscience, or the moral faculty. Both these are so far original parts of our constitution, that if there did not exist in every mind a sense of beauty and its contrary, and a sense of right and wrong, such ideas could be generated, or communicated by no process of education.

CHAPTER VII.

MORAL OBLIGATION.

Obligation.

MUCH has been written to explain the true ground of moral obligation. But the subject has been rather darkened and perplexed than elucidated, by these comments. It is always so when men undertake to explain that which is so clear that it needs no explanation.

Included in every idea of morality.

Every idea of morality includes in it that of moral obligation. A moral act is one which ought to be performed; an immoral act, is one which ought not to be performed. As soon as we get the conception of a moral act, we receive with it the idea of moral obligation. It would be a contradiction to say that any act was moral, and yet that there was no obligation to perform

11. One of the best definitions which can be given of a moral act, is that it is an act which we are bound to perform, and of an immoral act, that it is one which ought not to be done. The more clearly we see any thing to be moral, the more sensibly we feel ourselves under a moral obligation to perform it. This being a matter of common intuition, and universal experience, all that is necessary to convince us of its truth, is to bring it distinctly before our minds. There is therefore no need to look any further for the grounds and reasons of moral obligation, than to the morality of the act itself, as this idea is involved in every conception of morality.

What a moral act is.

The following citation from Dr. Price's work on Morals, is in accordance with the view just given: "From the account given of obligation, it appears how absurd it is to inquire, what *obliges* us to practise virtue? as if obligation were no part of the idea of virtue, but something adventitious and foreign to it: that is, as if what was our duty might not be our duty; as if it might

Why we are obliged to do right—not to be asked.

not be true, that what is *fit* to do, we *ought* to do, and that what we ought to do, we are obliged to do. To ask *why* we are *obliged* to practise virtue, to abstain from what is wicked, or perform what is just, is the very same as to ask why we are obliged to do what we are obliged to do. It is not possible to avoid wondering at those who have so unaccountably embarrassed themselves, on a subject that one would think was attended with so little difficulty: and who, because they cannot find any thing in virtue and duty themselves, which can induce and oblige us to pay a regard to them—fly to self-love, and maintain that from hence alone are derived all inducement and obligation."

Answer of Archdeacon Paley

Dr. Paley commences his second book on Moral Philosophy, by an inquiry into the nature of moral obligation. He asks, "Why am I obliged to keep my word?" and mentions several answers which would be given by different persons, and which he says all coincide. But he goes on to say that all the answers leave the matter short; for the inquirer may turn round upon his teacher with a second question, "Why am I obliged to do what is right, to act agreeably to the fitness of things, to conform to reason, nature or truth, to promote the public good, or to do the will of God?"

All this, it appears to us, is fitted to mystify as plain a subject as ever engaged the thoughts of a rational mind, and is designed to remove the true ground of Insufficient. moral obligation, and reduce all such obligation to the single principle of self-love, or the tendency of an act to promote individual happiness.

Suppose then, after Dr. Paley had made all obligation to rest on the ground that the performance of a good act promotes our eternal happiness, the inquirer The inquiry unreasonable. should again ask, "Why am I bound to perform that which will promote my happiness?" The question, indeed, would be unreasonable, because all men are agreed that happiness is a good; but is it not equally unreasonable, when an action is seen to be virtuous, or morally right, to ask "Why am I obliged to do it?" The moment we see a thing to be morally right, the sense of obligation is complete, and all further inquiring for reasons why I am obliged to do right is as absurd as would be inquiring for reasons why I should pursue happiness.

Where we have intuitive certainty of any thing it is foolish to seek for other reasons. If there is any thing clear in the view of a rational mind, it is this: that virtue should be practised, that what is right should be done. But still further to perplex this plain subject, Dr. Paley has undertaken to inform us what is meant by obligation. "A man," says he, "is said to be obliged when he is urged by a violent motive resulting from the will of another."

Intuitive certainty is ultimate.

This is, indeed, a very extraordinary definition. The motive, he says, must be violent; but what should hinder that a motive not violent should create an obligation according to its force? The main error of this definition is that it confounds moral obligation with other motives of

Paley's definition.

an entirely different kind. The obligation of which he speaks, is created by the will or command of another. The law of a tyrant requiring his subjects to do what is evidently wrong cannot create a moral obligation. A rational being may be urged by the threats of a tyrant, on the universal principle of self-love, and this force may, by an abuse of terms, be called an obligation; but according to the common usage of the language, when a man is said to be under obligation to perform an act, we mean that he is morally bound. But whether the operation of any violent motive, resulting from the will of another, may be said to oblige a man or not, the main inquiry is, what is the ground of moral obligation? The difference between a moral obligation and other motives which may oblige should be kept in view.

Paley's account of obligation.

He then returns to the question, "Why am I obliged to keep my word?" and applies the preceding definition of the nature of obligation, and gives the following answer: "Because I am urged to do so by a violent motive (namely, the expectation of being after this life rewarded if I do, or punished if I do not), resulting from the command of another (namely, of God)." He goes on to say, "When I first turned my attention to moral speculations, an air of mystery seemed to hang over the whole subject, which arose, I believe, from hence; that I supposed with many authors whom I had consulted that to be *obliged* to do a thing, was different from being *induced* to do it; and that the obligation to practise virtue, and to do what is justice, is quite another thing and of another kind from the obligation which a soldier is under to obey his officer, or a servant his master, or any of the ordinary obligations of human life."

We cannot but be of the opinion that Dr. Paley has here made a radical mistake, which it is exceedingly important to consider, since, unhappily for sound morals, his system is so much employed in the instruction of youth.

Erroneous.

The theory of morals, of which the above principle is a part, is no other than this: that the only difference between virtue and vice, consists in their tendency, respectively, to promote or hinder the happiness of the individual; so that if a man could persuade himself that no evil would arise to him from telling a lie, he would be under no obligation to speak the truth. It is a scheme of morals which obliterates all intrinsic difference between virtue and vice, and makes the one preferable to the other on no other account than its tendency to promote individual happiness in the future world.

Paley's scheme of morals.

If a man does not believe in a future world, he can, according to this theory, feel no obligation to keep his word. We believe, on the contrary, that moral obligation is felt by the atheist, and that he cannot divest himself of it. When men are tempted by some strong motive to deviate from the truth, and yet are enabled to resist the temptation, there is in most cases no distinct consideration of any future good to be gained by it, but the man feels himself under an obligation to do that which is in itself right. The conflict is not between a greater and a less

Difficulties of the hypothesis.

happiness, but between the prospect of happiness and moral obligation.

On this subject, the appeal must be to the common judgment of men. And we are persuaded that this confounding of moral obligation with motives of another kind, is a radical defect in Dr. Paley's system, which—lying at the foundation—vitiates the whole, and has already been the cause of great evil to society.

True doctrine stated.

The true doctrine is, that virtue and vice are distinct and opposite, and that when we know any act to be right, we are bound—aside from all considerations of self-interest—to perform it.

The opposite doctrine.

Dr. Paley maintains that "we can be obliged to nothing, unless we are to lose or gain something by it, for nothing else can be a 'violent motive' to us. And as we should not be obliged to obey the laws or the magistrate, unless rewards or punishments, pleasure or pain, somehow or other depended on our obedience; so neither should we, without the same reason, be obliged to do what is right, to practise virtue, or to obey the command of God."

According to this view, unless a man is persuaded that he shall gain something by keeping his word, he is under no obligation to do it. Even if God should clearly make known his will, and lay upon him his command, he is under no obligation to obey, unless certain that he shall receive benefit by so doing. This is, indeed, to make virtue a mercenary thing, and reduce all motives to a level. And as self-love, or the desire of happiness, is the only rational motive, and all men possess this in a sufficient degree of strength, the only conceivable difference between the good and the bad, consists in the superior sagacity which the one has above the other to discern what will most contribute to happiness. And if what we call vice or sin could be made to contribute to happiness, then it would change its nature and become virtue.

Virtue thus made mercenary.

The definition of obligation, given by Dr. Paley, upon his own principles, is unnecessarily encumbered with what adds nothing to its import. Why should the "violent motive" result from the command of another? The command of another ought to have no influence, except as obedience or disobedience will be attended with loss or gain. It would, therefore, have been more simple and intelligible to say at once, what is certainly implied, that the only motive which can oblige us to be virtuous, is the expectation of the happiness to be derived from such conduct in the future world.

Paley's definition obscure.

Cicero, in his work "De Finibus," says that those men who confounded the *honestum* with the *utile*, deserved to be banished from society. The result of the whole scheme is, that there is no such thing as moral excellence, abstractly considered; that the only good in the universe is happiness; and that other things, among which virtue is included, are good only as related to this end. If this is true, the moral attributes of God have no intrinsic excellence; they are all merged in his infinite felicity. Surely this view

The *honestum* and the *utile*.

is not suited to increase our reverence for the Supreme Being.

But every man who carefully examines into his own primary ideas of morality, will find that he has a sense of right and wrong, independent of all considerations of personal happiness, or its loss. This distinction is too deeply engraven on the mind to be erased by any process of reasoning.

Appeal to primary ideas.

CHAPTER VIII.

THE SUPREMACY OF CONSCIENCE.

Conscience must be obeyed.

THAT the dictates of conscience should be obeyed, is one of the most evident perceptions of the human mind. No matter how much might be gained by going contrary to conscience, every honest mind has the same judgment, that duty should be done. If it is plain that a certain act—such as confessing the truth of the gospel—is a duty, and we are convinced that nothing but suffering will ensue from performing it; yet the judgment of the impartial mind is, that no prospect of pain or loss can ever justify us in denying the truth, or in doing any thing else that we know to be wrong. On this point, there is no room for reasoning. The judgment that conscience should be obeyed, is intuitive:

all men must acknowledge it, unless they belie the clear convictions of their own reason.

That conscience should be obeyed, that duty should be performed at every risk, are maxims which must receive the assent of all who are capable of understanding them. On the subject of the supremacy of conscience, the following quotation from Dr. Chalmers, is very much to our purpose:

Admitted maxim.

"In every human heart there is a faculty—not, it may be, having the actual power, but having the just and rightful pretension to act as judge and master over the whole of human conduct. Other propensities may have too much sway, but the moral propensity—if I may so term it—never can; for, to have the presiding sway in all our concerns, is just that which properly and legitimately belongs to it. A man under anger, may be too strongly prompted to deeds of retaliation, or under sensuality may be too strongly prompted to indulgence, or under avarice, be too closely addicted to the pursuit of wealth, or even under friendship be too strongly inclined to

Chalmers

partiality; but he never can, under conscience, be too strongly inclined to be as he ought, and to do as he ought. We may say of a watch, that its main-spring is too powerful, but we would never say that a regulator was too powerful." . . . . "And neither do we urge the proposition that conscience has in every instance the actual direction of human affairs, for this were in the face of all experience. It is not that every man obeys her dictates, but that every man feels that he ought to obey them. These dictates are often, in life and practice, disregarded; so that conscience is not the sovereign *de facto.* Still there is a voice within the hearts of all which asserts that conscience is the sovereign *de jure:* that to her belongs the command rightfully, even though she do not possess it actually." . . . . "All that we affirm is, that if conscience prevail over the other principles, then every man is led, by the very make and mechanism of his internal economy, to feel, that it is as it ought to be; or if these others prevail over conscience, that it is not as it ought to be." . . . .

Conscience is sovereign.

"When stating the supremacy of conscience, in the sense that we have explained it, we but state what all men feel; and our only argument in proof of the assertion is—our only argument can be, an appeal to the experience of all men."

These sentiments will find a response in every honest mind. However often we disobey the voice of this monitor, we always have the feeling of self-condemnation accompanying our disobedience.

Inward verdict.

CHAPTER IX.

WHETHER WE ALWAYS DO RIGHT BY OBEYING THE DICTATES OF CONSCIENCE?

Difficulty of the problem.

THIS is one of the most perplexing questions in the science of morals. Many are of opinion that all that is necessary to render an action good is that the agent act agreeably to the dictates of his own conscience. This may be considered a vulgar opinion, usually taken up without much consideration. But there is an opinion, near akin to this, which has been advocated by some of the greatest men of the age; namely, that men are not responsible for their opinions or belief. It is thought that the adoption of this as a maxim is the only effectual method of putting an end to the bitter animosities and controversies among the advocates of different creeds.

It is not wonderful that they who make the moral sense, in a sort, infallible, and the ultimate standard of right and wrong, should hold that men cannot go astray if they will honestly listen to the voice of conscience, and obey her dictates.

Source of error.

But as we have shown that conscience is the judgment of the mind respecting duty, and as no man's knowledge is perfect or infallible, it follows, therefore, that so far as there is error in the understanding in relation to matters of duty, just so far the conscience will be misguided. The question at issue, therefore, is whether an action, wrong in itself, can be considered as a good and virtuous action if the agent believes that it is right. If the affirmative were true, then the discovery of truth would be of no value, for obviously upon this principle error is just as good as truth. But as soon would we believe that darkness is as good as light to direct us in the way which we wish to travel. Again, this theory supposes that a man is under

Error of understanding may affect moral judgments.

Otherwise truth would be needless.

no law but his own opinion, or the dictates of conscience; that, therefore, which is a sin in one man may be a duty to another in precisely the same external circumstances and relations; which would be to confound all moral distinctions.

Opinion would be law.

This theory would go to sanction every form of religion, however corrupt and superstitious; and to make the vilest immoralities virtuous; for there can be no doubt that the votaries of idolatry, in their most cruel and abominable rites, follow the dictates of an erring conscience. When the heathen sacrifice to demons, and when the victim is a human being, or even a first-born son, there is nothing wrong, for all these acts of worship are performed in obedience to conscience. Every species of persecution and the Inquisition itself may be justified on this principle. Instead, therefore, of putting an end to all animosity, it would bring back, in all their horrors, the days of persecution for conscience' sake.

False religion would be right.

On this subject, again, our appeal must be to the unbiassed judgment of mankind; and we think the verdict will be, that error which might have been avoided, and ignorance, which is not invincible, do not excuse. The knowledge necessary to duty is within the reach of every man, were he disposed sincerely to seek after it. But it is a truth which is of importance on this subject, that one false step leads to another; and though a man who has adopted fundamental error, labours under a kind of necessity to do wrong, yet this does not excuse him, because he ought to have exercised more diligence and impartiality in seeking for the truth, and is justly liable to all the evil consequences resulting from this neglect.

Avoidable and unavoidable.

Suppose a man to have been educated in a wrong system of religion and morals; he is responsible, because, when arrived at the years of maturity, he should have brought the opinions received by education under an honest examination. The more difficult it is to divest ourselves of prejudices thus imbibed, as it were, with the mother's milk, the more necessary is it that, under the in-

Duty of correcting errors.

fluence of a sincere love of truth, we should, with impartiality, diligence, and resolution, endeavour to do so. It is no proof that such a course is not the solemn duty of man, that few ever perform it. The prevalence of error in the world, is very much owing to the neglect of this duty. This neglect arises from culpable indolence, from a desire to remain in agreement with the multitude or with our parents and teachers, from aversion to the truth and an unwillingness to deny ourselves, and incur the inconvenience and persecution which an avowal of the truth would bring upon us. But none of these reasons will justify us in adhering to opinions which are detrimental to ourselves and others, or contrary to our moral obligations. It is true, if a man's conscience dictates a certain action, he is morally bound to obey; but if that action is in itself wrong, he commits sin in performing it, nevertheless. He who is under fundamental error, is in a sad dilemma. Do what he will, he sins. If he disobey conscience, he knowingly sins; doing what he believes to be wrong; and a man never can be justified for doing what he believes to be wrong, even though it should turn out to be right. And if he obey conscience, performing an act which is in itself wrong, he sins; because he complies not with the law under which he is placed. It may be asked, "How can a man be responsible in such circumstances, when he is under a necessity of doing wrong?" We are responsible for suffering ourselves to be brought into such a state; we are responsible for our ignorance of the truth. Hence we see how important the duty of seeking after truth with untiring diligence, and honest impartiality. The same necessity is found to arise from forming bad habits, and cherishing evil passions. The heart in which envy to another has been indulged until it has become habitual, cannot exercise kind and brotherly affections to that person; but this is no excuse. The fault may be traced far back, but guilt is attached to every act of envy, however inveterate the habit. If this were not so, the greater the sinner, the less his responsibility.

The seat of responsibility in such a case.

The objection to making a man responsible for his opinions, is, that his belief does not depend upon his will, but results necessarily from the evidence existing before the mind, at any moment. This is true; but we may turn our minds away from the evidence which would have produced a conviction of the truth. And this is not all; there may be such a state of mind, that evidence of a certain kind cannot be perceived. Depravity produces blindness of mind, in regard to the beauty and excellency of moral objects. But every man ought to be free from such a state or temper of mind, as produces distorted or erroneous views. Surely, moral depravity cannot be an excuse for erroneous opinions. All actions proceed from certain principles; if, therefore, the action is wrong, because of the corrupt principle, the burden of culpability must be rolled back upon the principle, or state of the soul, which sends forth evil acts, as a poisoned fountain sends forth deleterious streams.

Objection, that belief is involuntary.

Metaphysical reasoning, however, rather perplexes and obscures than elucidates such points. Let us hold fast by the plain principles of common sense, and appeal to the common judgment of mankind; and the decision will be, that ignorance or error which might have been avoided, never excuses from blame. The same is true of all evil habits and inveterate passions, which have been voluntarily or heedlessly contracted. The whole course of a moral agent must be taken together; his moral acts are complicated, and intimately connected. They form a web, in which one thread is connected with another, and one serves to give strength to another. If we honestly consult our conscience, we feel guilty when we have done wrong, even though we did it ignorantly; because we ought not to have been in ignorance.

Avoidable ignorance does not excuse.

Two things, therefore, are necessary, in order to determine that an action is right: first, that the state of mind of the agent be such as it ought to be; and secondly, that the action be in conformity with the law under which we are placed; for the very idea of morality supposes us to be under a moral law.

What constitutes a right action.

While, then, we cannot do better than obey

conscience; yet if conscience is erroneous, we do not fulfil our duty by such obedience, but may commit grievous sin.

Duty not fulfilled by obeying erroneous conscience.

For, following the dictates of conscience, is only one circumstance essential to a good action. When we do wrong while obeying the dictates of conscience, the error does not consist in that obedience, but in not following the right rule, with which rule the accountable moral agent should be acquainted.

CHAPTER X.

WHETHER THERE IS IN THE MIND A LAW OR RULE, BY WHICH MAN JUDGES OF THE MORALITY OF PARTICULAR ACTIONS?

If such a rule existed in the mind prior to the observation of particular acts of a moral nature, we should be conscious of it: nothing of the nature of a law or rule can have existence in the mind, without the knowledge of the mind itself.

Mental rules are objects of consciousness.

There seems to be a common mistake as to the process of the mind in regard to general principles. It seems to be thought that in order to judge whether an action be right or wrong, there must be something like a general rule or law, which the mind applies, as the workman does

The actual process of the mind in moral judgments.

his rule, to ascertain whether the quality of the action be good or bad. But as we are conscious of no such process as the application of a general rule, there seems to be no evidence whatever of its existence. The real process of the mind is very simple. When a moral action is viewed, if its nature is simple and palpable, the mind intuitively perceives its quality, and is conscious of no other mental process. Suppose a man, created as Adam was, in the full possession of his rational faculties: until some occasion offered, to elicit its exercise, he would not be conscious of any moral faculty or feeling. But suppose an act of flagrant injustice to be perpetrated before him, he would at once have his moral faculty brought into exercise. He would see that the action had in it a moral turpitude, that it ought not to have been done, and that the agent deserved to be punished. So long as this was the only moral act observed or thought of, there would be in the mind nothing but the judgment, with the accompanying feeling that such an act, and of course every other act of the same kind, was evil. As such an observer would, however, soon observe a multitude of acts, of different kinds, which were judged to be good or bad, a general rule or law would be obtained, by degrees, out of these particulars. The process of the mind, in all cases, is from particulars to generals, and the tendency in the mind to put into classes those things which resemble each other, exists also in regard to moral actions. After observing a great number of acts, of different kinds, all of which are morally good or evil, these particulars are classified, and form a general rule or law; and when a new act is observed, it is referred to its proper class. But how can we know an action to be good or bad, without a rule with which to compare it, in the first instance? The answer is, that it is as easy to conceive of a faculty by which we can at once perceive the moral character of an act, as of the power of judging of the rectitude of a general rule.

There is a sense in which it may be said, that reason, or the moral faculty having the power of discerning the moral quality of actions, has the rule in itself. If this is all that is intended by a general rule of right and wrong in the mind, there can be no objection to it. This is saying no more than that the mind has a faculty by which it judges intuitively of many moral acts, as soon as they are observed. The idea may be thus illustrated: here is a straight line, as soon as I see it, I perceive it to be straight; there is a crooked line, which at once I perceive to be crooked. There is no need of a rule in the mind, by the application of which I know that the one is straight, and the other crooked. The quality of the lines is seen at once. So of many moral actions, the moment the mind apprehends them, their moral character is perceived.

Whether the moral faculty has the rule in itself.

Here are some boys going to school. I observe one, who is large and strong, forcibly taking from another, who is small and weak, some fruit which the latter has with much pains gathered for a sick mother. I need no general rule to guide my judgment. I need only to know the real circumstances of the action. That a large and strong boy should by force take away from one

A case stated.

weaker than himself, property to which he has no right, and to which the other has a right, is so evidently immoral, that every mind sees the vil at once.

The general law or rule of morals is therefore made up by the observation and classification of particular acts; just as the general law of gravity is formed by observation of particular facts.

General law of morals from particular acts.

All our knowledge relates originally to particular cases; and general ideas and general rules and laws, are formed by a process of the mind, which may be called generalization or classification.

Analogy of other generalizations.

CHAPTER XI.

THE MORAL FEELING WHICH ACCOMPANIES EVERY MORAL JUDGMENT.

Feelings of approbation and disapprobation.

WHETHER our judgments and feelings are distinct and separate mental exercises, or whether what we call feeling or emotion is only an idea of a more vivid kind, is a question which we need not discuss, as the decision of it is not necessary to our purpose. All men make a distinetion between acts which are purely intellectual, and those exercises of mind called emotions; and no practical error can arise from observing this distinction—whether philosophically correct or not. In every case where a moral object or relation comes before the mind, there is a feeling of approbation or disapprobation, according to the moral character of the object, of which we are immediately conscious. This approbation or disapprobation will not be equal in all cases, but exceedingly different in degree. While some moral actions elicit, when perceived, a very slight degree of approbation or disapprobation, others excite strong emotion; the disapproval arising to indignation, and the approval to admiration.

In every instance where a good act is observed, there is a feeling of esteem for the agent, as well as approbation of the act.

The idea of merit.

A disposition, too, is felt to bestow some reward on the person who performs a good action. If we see a man, at the imminent risk of his own life, plunge into the sea to save a stranger who has fallen overboard, we approve the action, and feel that he deserves a reward. We therefore call it a meritorious action; for the simple idea of merit is that which deserves a reward.

On the other hand, when we are witnesses of a wicked act of an enormous kind, as, for example, a man murdering a good parent or a kind benefactor, without any provocation, but instigated by avarice or resentment—we feel instantaneously a degree of disapprobation which may properly be called indignation. This feeling would be accompanied by a strong desire that condign punishment should be inflicted on the wicked perpetrator of such a deed. If there were no other means of executing justice, we should feel disposed to aid in punishing the culprit; and the idea of such a person escaping without punishment, is painful to the impartial mind, and revolting to the moral feelings.

The vindicatory feeling.

These moral emotions are, however, of very different degrees of intensity in different persons, and in the same person at different periods of his life. Persons who have been long accustomed to see atrocious crimes committed, lose in time their moral sensibility, and become accustomed to scenes of blood and robbery. In proportion as the minds of men are enlightened by the truth, and their hearts upright, will be the sensibility of the moral faculty. But by committing sin, as well as by observing it, the

Degrees in moral emotions.

moral sensibilities are blunted. This want of right feeling in the conscience is what is called a "seared conscience," which expression is borrowed from the effect produced on any part of a living body, by the repeated application of a heated iron. The result is, that, by degrees, the skin thickens, and the sensibility of the seared part is lost, or rendered obtuse.

Besides this feeling of approbation or disapprobation of moral acts, good or evil, there is a peculiar emotion, in relation to moral acts, according to their nature, when performed by ourselves. In this case, the emotion is much more vivid than when we contemplate the same action as performed by another. When a person is conscious of having performed a truly good action, and from the proper motives, he experiences an emotion of pleasure, of a very peculiar and exalted nature For this emotion, we have no distinctive name; it may be called the pleasure of a good or approving conscience. It must not be confounded with self-complacency, or a proud opinion of our own worth, which may also arise from the per-

Emotion in regard to acts as our own.

formance of a meritorious action. The feeling of which mention has been made, is a simple emotion arising in the mind, from the principles of the human constitution, upon the performance of a good action. One reason why it has not been more noticed is, that it has no distinctive name. The emotion experienced on the performance of a wicked action is well known to every one. It has a distinctive appellation—*remorse.* It is a feeling distinguishable from all others, and more intolerable than any other species of pain. When violent, it often drives the unhappy subject of it to the most desperate acts. It is like a scorpion, stinging the soul in its tenderest part. No language can exaggerate the misery of a soul abandoned to the torture of this feeling. And though in time it may seem to be allayed by forgetfulness of the crime, yet when any circumstance or association brings the evil action distinctly before the conscience, the torment is renewed. Thus, acts of iniquity committed in heedless gayety, often produce sensible remorse in the time of solitude and reflection; and the sins of youth embitter old age. This feeling often accompanies the sinner to his times of decline, and is the pain which most annoys him on his bed of death. As the feeling accompanies the guilty unto the last moment of their earthly existence, there is much reason to think that it will cause the bitterest anguish of a future state.

CHAPTER XII.

BELIEF IN GOD, AS CONNECTED WITH THE OPERATION OF CONSCIENCE.

THE question is, whether an atheist is completely divested of the feeling of moral obligation. To those who suppose that speculative atheism is impossible, this question will appear irrelevant; for it would be useless to inquire what would be the effect of a state of mind which never can exist.

The question stated.

As, however, the evidences of the actual existence of atheism are as strong as those of most other fundamental errors; and as the doctrine of certain ideas being impressed on the mind in its creation (on which the opinion that men could not become atheists was founded), is now generally exploded, it may be here taken as admitted that there are atheists in the world.

The atheist perceives right and wrong.

The question proposed is therefore a proper subject for consideration. Bishop Warburton in his "Divine Legation of Moses," seems to adopt the opinion, that a belief in the being of God, is requisite to the exercise of conscience, or the sense of moral obligation. But his reasonings on the subject are by no means satisfactory. If we may refer to the experience of the atheist himself, he will assure us, that he perceives the difference between right and wrong, as plainly as others, and that he is conscious of being under a moral obligation to pursue a virtuous course. This, however, they consider an instinctive or constitutional principle, which should be obeyed, just as our appetites and other natural propensities should be obeyed.

Intuitive perceptions not dependent on other knowledge.

If there are intuitive perceptions of moral relations, when actions of a certain kind are presented to the view of the rational mind, then it is certain that conscience may and will operate, whatever may be the opinions of the person on other subjects. No one, when he contemplates an act of flagrant injustice, is conscious of a reference to the existence of a moral Governor, prior to his moral judgment of the quality of the action. The perception of its moral evil is as immediate as that of the colour of the sky, or the grass. But how can a man feel a moral obligation, unless he admits that there is a superior to whom he is bound? how can he feel himself under a law, unless there is a law-giver? The answer is, that this part of the human constitution furnishes a conclusive argument in favour of the being of God. We have a law written within us, and from the sense of obligation to obey this law, we cannot escape. The great Creator has not left himself without a witness, in the breast of every man. It is possible that a man may be so abandoned as to believe in lies, and that he may come to disbelieve in the God that made and supports him. But he cannot obliterate the law written on his heart; he cannot divest himself of the conviction that certain actions are morally wrong; nor can he prevent the stings of remorse, when he commits sins of an enormous kind. Men may, indeed, spin out refined meta-

Objection and answer.

physical theories, and come to the conclusion that there is no difference between virtue and vice, and that these distinctions are the result of education. But let some one commit a flagrant act of injustice toward themselves, and their practical judgment will give the lie to their theoretical opinion.

Moral distinctions cannot be reasoned away

As those speculatists who argue that there is no external world, will avoid running against a post, or into the fire, as carefully as other men; so they who endeavour to reason themselves into the belief that virtue and vice are mere notions, generated by education, cannot, nevertheless, avoid perceiving that some actions are base, unjust, or ungrateful, and consequently to be disapproved of, whether committed by themselves or others.

Conscience cannot be destroyed.

The inferences from what has been said are, that by no arts or course of conduct can men so eradicate the moral faculty, that there shall no longer be any sense of right and wrong. And again, it is evident that, although the belief of the existence of God is not necessary to the operations of conscience, yet from the existence of this faculty the existence of God may be inferred.

And finally, that although the atheist cannot destroy the moral faculty, yet the firmer the belief of God's existence, and the clearer the knowledge of his attributes, the more distinct and forcible will be the dictates of conscience. Moreover, while the blindness of atheism continues, there will of course be no perception of the moral duties which arise out of our relation to the great Creator; and thus the largest and most important class of moral actions will be out of view. And this is true, to a great degree, in regard to the practical atheist, who forgets God habitually; he feels very little sense of obligation to worship and serve him.

Dictates of conscience modified by belief in God.

CHAPTER XIII.

MORAL AGENCY, AND WHAT IS NECESSARY TO IT.

The question to be determined by experience

As actions of moral agents are the proper and only objects of moral approbation or disapprobation, it becomes necessary to institute an inquiry into the nature of moral agency; or into what are the constituents of a moral agent. The decision of this question must depend entirely on experience, and can never be determined by reasoning on abstract principles. The process is simply this: we contemplate a great variety of acts, which by the moral faculty we judge to possess a moral character. We next examine the circumstances in which those acts were performed, and we conclude those things which are found in all of them, to be necessary to moral agency. Or, to render the examination more simple, we may suppose some one condition of the action to be absent, and then another, and then viewing the action as thus changed in its circumstances, we may bring it before the mind, and if the moral quality of the act appear unchanged, we conclude that that which has been removed from it is no essential circumstance in moral agency. But if the change in the circumstances of the action, leads all men to take an entirely different view of its nature, then we conclude that this circumstance is essential to moral agency.

Instance touching moral agency. To illustrate this principle, let us suppose the following case: If we see a man suddenly, without any apparent provocation, raise his hand and strike another, believing that it was freely done, by a man *compos mentis*, we feel a strong disapprobation of the act, as immoral and deserving punishment. But if on inquiry it is ascertained that the person who committed the assault was utterly destitute of reason, we may blame his keepers or friends who left him at liberty, but we no longer feel any moral disapprobation of the act. For it is the intuitive judgment of all persons, that a man destitute of reason is not a moral agent, nor accountable for his actions, whatever evil may be produced. We consider such a man as exactly in the same predicament as a wild beast which does an injury. This is the common judgment of men; for in all courts of justice, when a man is arraigned for an assault, if it can be proved that he was a maniac at the time, he is acquitted, and all men approve the judicial decision which exempts him from punishment. Hence it is apparent that the exercise of reason is essential to moral agency. We may bring before our minds a thousand acts, under different circumstances, but all performed by agents without reason, and no man can believe that such actions are of a moral nature, or of good or ill desert.

Exercise of reason indispensable.

It may seem to be an objection to this broad assertion that there are some who entertain the opinion that infants are moral agents from their birth, and commit actual sin. But these persons do not suppose that an irrational being can be a

No objection lies, from the case of infants.

moral agent, but they think that infants have an obscure exercise of reason. Their mistake is not in the general principle which has been laid down, but in the fact that infants have reason in exercise.

Again, let the case supposed be varied. Let it be that the person committing the assault had the full exercise of reason, but that the stroke was not voluntary, but the effect of a spasmodic, diseased, action of the muscles; or that the hand was moved by another. Every one, at once, judges that the person giving the stroke, whatever he might be in other matters, was no moral agent in this assault. It was a mere physical operation, and not proceeding from the will, could not be a moral act. Here we have a second circumstance or characteristic, essential to moral agency, namely, that the action be voluntary. No involuntary action can be of a moral nature.

Another instance.

Voluntary action necessary.

Some distinguish the liberty of the agent from voluntariness, but to us they appear to be the same, or to involve one another. If an act is voluntary, it is free; and if free, it must be voluntary. The highest conceivable degree of liberty in a dependent being, is the power of doing as he wills or pleases. But as this subject has by metaphysical controversy been involved in perplexity, something may be said hereafter, respecting what is called the freedom of the will.

Liberty and voluntariness.

When it is said that the actions of moral agents are the only proper objects of moral approbation or disapprobation, two qualifications of the assertion must be taken into view. The first is, that the omission to act when duty calls, is as much an object of disapprobation as a wicked action. Should we see a number of persons sailing on a river in a boat, and while we surveyed them, should a child near them fall into the river, and no hand be stretched out to rescue it from drowning, we could not help feeling a strong disapprobation of the conduct of the persons who were near enough to render the necessary help. If, however, it should be ascertained

Omission may be culpable.

that one or more of the persons were fast bound and pinioned, so that they could not possibly stretch out their hands to rescue the child, we should exempt them from all blame: for no man is bound to do what is physically impossible. The second qualification of the statement is, that when we disapprove an external act, we always refer the blame to the motive or intention.

Blame is referred to the intent.

But if we have evidence that the agent possesses a nature or disposition which will lead him often or uniformly to perpetrate the same act when the occasion shall occur, we not only censure the motive, but extend our moral disapprobation to the disposition or evil nature, lying behind.

If we suppose the case of an agent acted on by a superior power, so that the nature and direction of the act depend not upon the agent himself, but upon the power by which he is governed, we shall consider the immediate agent as not free, and the acts brought forth, as not properly his acts, but those of the governing power. A demoniac or person possessed by an evil spirit

Acts under control.

who had power to direct his thoughts and govern his actions, would not be an accountable agent.

There are some who maintain that all human actions proceed from God, as their first cause, and that man can act only as he is acted upon. Upon this theory, it does not appear how man can be an accountable moral agent; for though his actions may be voluntary, and performed in the exercise of reason, yet as he does not originate them, they can scarcely be considered his own.

Divine efficiency in human acts.

We will now suppose the case of a man possessing reason, freedom, and will, and originating his own actions, but destitute of a moral faculty, or unable to perceive a difference between right and wrong. Can such a person be considered a moral agent? We think not. That being—how much soever of reason he may possess—who has no perception of moral relations, and no feeling of moral obligation, would be incapable of a moral law, or of performing moral acts. But the case is an imaginary one. There are, I

Moral faculty necessary to moral agency.

believe, none, who possess reason, and yet are destitute of all moral sense; but though we conceive of the intellect of a dog or an elephant increased to any degree, yet, as being destitute of a moral faculty, we do not regard them as moral agents.

CHAPTER XIV.

MAN A MORAL AGENT.

VERY few have entertained the opinion that man is a mere machine, governed by physical influences. It will not be necessary, therefore, to occupy time in refuting an opinion contrary to reason and universal experience.

The question stated.

But there are many who entertain the opinion that man is the creature of necessity; that in the circumstances in which each man is placed, he could not be different from what he is. This theory of fatalism is plausible, because a slight observation of the history of man shows that the moral characters of most men are formed by the education which they receive, and by the sentiments and conduct of those with whom they associate.

Fatalism.

It has, therefore, been maintained—and the opinion has in our day been industriously propagated—that man is not a free and accountable agent; that he is what he is, by the operation of causes over which he has no control; that no man should be censured or punished for his conduct, since those who censure him, if placed in the same circumstances, would act in the same manner. In short, that no man is responsible for his conduct; because his actions—whether good or bad—are the effect of necessary causes. It is held by the same persons that the only possible method of meliorating the condition of the human race, is to educate them in such a manner as to avoid those prejudices which have hitherto proved inimical to the happiness of men; and to remodel society, rejecting those institutions which are supposed to cause most of the misery which is found in the world. This theory has not only been embraced with confidence, but attempts have been made to carry it out in practice. Societies founded on the principles above

The theory of circumstances.

Socialistic scheme.

stated, have been formed both in Great Britain and America. But thus far the experiment has been attended with small success. Still the advocates of the *Social system*, as it is called, have not been discouraged. They are instituting new societies upon an improved plan, and the most sanguine hopes are entertained by those concerned in these new associations, that a far better and happier state of society than any hitherto enjoyed, is practicable and will be realized.

Consciousness declares man free.

In answer to all arguments brought to prove that man is not a free moral agent, we appeal to the consciousness of every rational being. No arguments, however plausible, are of any force against intuitive first principles. Whether we can or cannot answer arguments against liberty, we know that we are free. In regard to some actions, we feel that we are under a moral obligation to perform them, and in regard to others, that we ought not to perform them, and if we are induced to violate this obligation, we feel that we are to be blamed, and are deserving of punishment.

Some philosophers have been persuaded by their reasonings that man is not free, but under necessity in all his actions. But as they could not deny that every man is intimately conscious of being free, they have adopted the opinion that man's feeling of liberty is a deceptive feeling, and contrary to fact. A far more reasonable conclusion is that there must be some error in the reasoning from which the conclusion that man is not a free agent, is deduced. When a chain of reasoning brings us to conclusions repugnant to our intuitive convictions, it is certain that there is a flaw in some link of it, whether we can discover it or not. We are as certain that we are free, as we can be; a revelation from heaven could not render us more so. As in other instances where speculative men have been led to adopt conclusions at variance with self-evident principles, so here, men act, in common life, in con formity with the common notions of mankind. They can by no effort divest themselves of this assent to certain fundamental truths.

This consciousness not deceptive.

CHAPTER XV.

MAN NOT UNDER A FATAL NECESSITY.

Arguments of Fatalism.

ALTHOUGH our consciousness of freedom ought to satisfy us, whatever reasonings to the contrary may be adduced; yet it may be useful to inquire whether, indeed, there are any arguments of force against the free agency of man. It is certain that one truth cannot be in opposition to any other truth. If, therefore, the deductions of reason and the evident principles of common sense and experience seem to stand in opposition to one another, it must arise from some misapprehension, or abuse of terms. As our understanding is given us to enable us to apprehend truth, no proposition clearly perceived to be true, whether intuitively or by ratiocination, can possibly be opposed to any other truth.

Notion of Liberty and Necessity.

It becomes necessary, therefore, in the first place, to have distinct ideas of what is meant by liberty, and what by necessity. Here the reference must be not to metaphysical reasoning, but to the common judgment and clear conviction of all impartial men. It has already been stated that that liberty which is necessary to moral agency, can be nothing else than the liberty of doing what we will, to the extent of our power. It is freedom of action in conformity with our desire and will. When a man is compelled by force to strike another (I mean not by the force of strong motives, but by actual physical force), we say he is not accountable, because not free to do as he willed. When we think of that liberty which is necessary to free agency, and to the performance of a moral act, this is the kind of liberty which we have in our minds. In judging of the moral quality of an act, we never attempt to go further back than the spontaneous inclination of the mind, and never think it necessary to know in what way this disposition was acquired. If the action proceed from will, so far as liberty is concerned it is a moral act. We cannot conceive of any greater or more desirable liberty than this. Dependent creatures, indeed, cannot possess that independent liberty which is the prerogative of the Deity. The creature, notwithstanding his liberty, is still under the government of divine providence.

The necessity which precludes free agency.

It is also important that we entertain distinct and accurate ideas of that necessity which is inconsistent with free agency. There is what has been termed moral or philosophical necessity, which is not incompatible with human liberty. This is no other than the certain operation of moral causes, producing moral effects, according to the power which they possess. Such necessity, it has been shown, must belong to God, because he cannot act in opposition to truth, wisdom, and justice. But this does not hinder him from acting freely. So the angels in heaven and glorified saints are so confirmed in holiness that they cannot sin; but still in loving and serving God they act most freely.

Incorrect use of the term necessary.

But as in the common use of terms, and according to the common apprehension of men, liberty and necessity are diametrically opposite; when the name necessity is applied to any exercise, the prejudice immediately arises that it cannot be free; especially if there be some points in which it coincides with real necessity. Here, it is probable, we have the true source of the difficulty and perplexity in which this subject has been involved. The word necessary should never have been applied to any exercises which are spontaneous or voluntary, because all such are free in their very nature. When we apply this term to them, although we may qualify it by calling it a moral or philosophical necessity, still the idea naturally and insensibly arises, that if necessary they cannot be free. It is highly important not to use a term out of its proper signification; especially when such consequences may arise from an ambiguous use. An event may be absolutely certain without being neces sary. It was absolutely certain that God, in creating the world, would act most wisely. It is a matter of absolute certainty that the holy angels will continue to love and serve God incessantly; but this certainty is not inconsistent with liberty. If a man possess good principles, and all temptation to do wrong be removed, it is morally certain that, in any given case, he will do right; and if a man be of corrupt principles, and all virtuous considerations be foreign from his thoughts, and strong temptations be presented to his ruling passion, it is certain that he will yield to temptation and commit sin. But in all these cases there is no necessity, because there is no coercion or compulsion. If the mere certainty of an event were inconsistent with freedom, then there could be no such thing as liberty in God or the creatures. As God knows all things most certainly, every thing, in his view, whatever may be its cause, is equally certain; the divine prescience cannot be mistaken. There is no good reason why uncertainty should be considered essential to that liberty which is necessary

Certainty not necessity.

to moral actions. All causes operate according to their nature and force. The reason why one effect is necessary and another free is not that the one takes place without an adequate cause or that the same cause may produce different effects; for both these are contrary to common sense. The true reason is that the one is produced against will, or without will, whereas the other is a voluntary act.

Importance of the distinction.

Let the distinction between what is certain and what is necessary be fully comprehended and attended to, and a great part of the darkness which, in the view of many, has obscured this subject will be dissipated. Although, then, it should be demonstrated that the will is as certainly governed by motives as the scale of the balance is by weights, yet there can be no legitimate inference from the one to the other, as if that would prove that the will is not free but under a necessity. The difference lies not in the difference of certainty in the two cases, but in the difference in the nature of the causes of that certainty.

CHAPTER XVI.

MAN'S DIRECTION AND GOVERNMENT OF HIS ACTIONS, AND HIS CONSEQUENT RESPONSIBILITY.

Extremes to be avoided.

THERE are two extremes to be avoided here. The first is that which considers man as, in some sense, a passive recipient of influences from without. He is represented as placed in certain circumstances and surrounded by certain objects, in the selection of which he has had no choice; and as he is susceptible of certain impressions which these circumstances and objects are fitted to make upon him, he cannot be considered a free and accountable agent.

In opposition to this false hypothesis we assert that the whole force which governs man is within, and proceeds from himself. External objects are in themselves inert. They exert no influence; no power emanates from them. The only power and influence which they can possibly have over any man they derive from the active principles of his nature. We are, indeed, accustomed in popular language to say that external objects excite and inflame the mind; but in philosophical accuracy they are but the passive objects on which the affections and desires of the mind fasten, and their whole power of moving to action depends upon the strength of the inward affections of the soul. To render this perfectly plain to every mind, it will only be necessary to attend to a few familiar illustrations.

The power really from within.

To a man who is under the influence of hunger or thirst, bread and water are said, when seen, greatly to excite him, so that he is strongly impelled to appropriate these objects to the craving wants of his nature. But every one sees at once that both the bread and the water are merely passive objects on which the appetite fixes. The real force which impels to action, is not, therefore, the external object, but the inward desire

No force in outward objects.

which is in the soul itself. For where no appetite of hunger or thirst exists, the bread and water, however presented and urged upon the sense, produce no effect; there is no motive to action experienced.

Take another case. A man comes into a room where lies a pile of gold. Avarice urges him to seize the beloved object, and appropriate it to himself. Two desires or motives counteract the tendency of avarice; one is a sense of duty or regard to the dictate of conscience, which he knows ought to be obeyed; the other is a regard to reputation, or the good opinion of men. Between these two antagonistical principles, there must of course be a conflict. If avarice be strong, and the power of conscience and desire of the good opinion of men be comparatively weak, the consequence will be that the man will put forth his hand and take the gold, and at the same time will feel conscious that he is doing wrong. But if conscience be fully awake, and especially if a love of moral excellence and a hatred of iniquity have a place in his mind,

Force resides in internal principles.

this motive alone will be sufficient to induce him to reject at once the thought of appropriating what belongs to another. In this case it is evident that the gold on the table is altogether passive; there is no secret emanation from the inert metal. The whole power of gold to seduce the mind to evil depends on the strength of the principle of avarice within; and in a mind rightly constituted, or under the influence of good moral dispositions, it could never so prevail as to induce the person to do an unlawful act for the sake of obtaining it.

Externals are only objects.

From these cases it is evident that a man is not governed by any influence from without or separate from himself, but that the true spring of his actions lies entirely in his own inclinations and will, external things having no other influence than as they furnish objects suited to his appetites and other desires.

Some writers on the will, in speaking of the governing power of motives, have expressed themselves in a manner which leads to the opinion that the motives by which the will is determined exist without us, or separate from ourselves, whereas those motives which possess an active power and govern our voluntary actions, are within us, and are our own active powers and affections, for which we are as responsible as for any other acts or operations of the mind. Hence it may truly be affirmed that every man possesses a self-determining power by which he regulates and governs his own actions according to his own inclinations.

Motives not separate existences.

The other extreme in regard to this subject is, that the will possesses a self-determining power in itself, independent of all motives, and uninfluenced by any inclination. And it is maintained that such a self-determining power is essential to freedom, and to the existence of an accountable moral agent. If, indeed, this last opinion were correct we should admit the self-determining power of the will, whether we understood its nature or not; for we lay it down as a first principle—from which we can no more depart than from the consciousness of existence—that MAN

Self-determining power.

IS FREE; and therefore stand ready to embrace whatever is fairly included in the definition of freedom. But it is not yet made evident, or even probable, that such a power exists, or that it is at all necessary to free moral agency, or that the possession of such a power would be valuable or desirable.

Not necessary.

All that is wanted is to make man the master of his own actions, and this is completely effected by giving him the power to will and act in accordance with his own inclinations. Certainly a man is not the less accountable for his actions because they are in accordance with his desires. Every rational being acts with a view to some end, and his regard or affection for that end is the motive which governs his will and influences his conduct.

Denial of such power does not conflict with liberty.

It cannot be justly denied, and is generally admitted, that in most cases the determinations of the will are influenced by strong desires; and when such desires exist, and there are none leading a contrary way, the decisions of the will are in fact determined by the previous state of the mind. Now if the prevalence of these desires in such cases is not found to interfere with free agency, there is no reason to think that the belief that the will is invariably determined by the strongest existing desire will lead to any conclusion unfavourable to liberty. If the self-determining power in question is exerted only in trivial cases where motives to action are weak, or when there is an equipoise of motives, it cannot be a power of any great consequence, since most of our moral acts are performed without its aid.

Instances examined.

Let us first take an impartial view of the acts of a man in the exercise of the power which all admit he possesses, and then of this imaginary power which some think essential to moral agency.

First case.

In the first case the man exercising his reason, apprehends objects which appear to him, on some account, good and desirable. These objects he desires to obtain, and puts forth those volitions which produce the actions requisite to the accomplishment of his object.

In the second case the man feels an inclination leading him with more or less force to a certain object; but he has a power which he can at any time exert to arrest his action in the line of his inclinations, and by exerting this power of willing he can counteract any desire, and act in opposition to it. Or if two desires exist, he can by this power give the prevalence to that which is the weaker. The best way to bring this matter to the test of experience is to suppose a case in which such a power is exerted. Suppose the case of a man in whom, by habit and indulgence, the appetite for intoxicating drink is strong; but he is induced by weighty reasons derived from a sense of duty and a regard to his health, reputation, family, and temporal prosperity, to determine not to expose himself to temptation. An old companion calls and solicits him to go with him to a convivial meeting. His appetite strongly pleads for indulgence, if only for this one time; but conscience remonstrates, and a regard to health, reputation, and the like, operates strongly on the other side. Suppose the influence felt

Second case.

from these two opposite sources to be almost equally balanced; suppose even a perfect equipoise. Such a state of mind, though possible and frequently experienced, can never last long, for the states of the mind change in some respects every moment, and the least difference in the views of the subject would destroy the balance. But now is the time for the exercise of the power which determines without regard to motive. Suppose, while the scales are thus in equipoise, this power to be exerted, and the man determines in favour of self-denial. Why he did thus determine, seems to be a reasonable inquiry; but if this power exists, such a question is entirely irrelative. There was, according to the supposition, no reason or motive which influenced the determination. Here then is a case for our consideration: Is an action prompted by no motive, and performed without a view to any end, an accountable moral act? If this self-determining power exists, it may be exerted in opposition to the highest and best motives, and neither the person himself nor any body else can tell why it was exerted. If a man under the influence of love to his Creator, should be about to engage in the performance of some plain and important duty, the exertion of this power at the most unseasonable time might arrest his action and lead him to a contrary determination. Why would he exert such a power at such a time? That, indeed, is the question. But if any reason of any kind could be given it would destroy the hypothesis, which is that a man has power to determine in opposition to all existing motives, and where there is a competition can act in conformity with the weakest. Surely such a power is irrational and dangerous in the extreme, and has no tendency to increase that freedom which is requisite to a moral agent.

No power to determine against all motives.

CHAPTER XVII.

OBJECTIONS TO THE UNIFORM INFLUENCE OF MOTIVES.

ONE of the most plausible objections to the uniform influence of motives on the will is, the intimate conviction every man has, when he has done what he regrets, that he could have done otherwise; whereas, upon the hypothesis laid down above, the man could not possibly, with the same motives, have acted differently from what he did. And it is alleged that no man ever would or could repent of his most criminal conduct, were he persuaded that he could not have willed and acted differently from what he did.

Objection from regret at wrong actions.

This objection brings out the true issue in this inquiry. The real question in dispute in regard to the will is, whether, all things external and internal being the same to any voluntary agent, the volitions will be the same. That is, whether a man in the same state of mind and under the influence of the same desires and motives, in kind and degree, will not always will and act in the same way. This we affirm; and the advocates of the self-determining power of the will, deny.

The true question stated.

It is admitted that when a man has done wrong and is convinced of his error, he is deeply conscious that he might and should have acted differently. But when this conviction is analyzed, it is found to be, not that he might have willed and acted differently with the same feelings that influenced him at the moment of doing wrong, but that he might and should have had a different state of feeling, or a more considerate attention to those things which were forgotten, but which if recollected would have prevented him from doing that which he now regrets.

Analysis of the alleged conviction.

Take a case. A man in an hour of levity, and under the influence of a degree of envy, speaks disrespectfully of a person whose character is worthy of esteem, and to whom he is under special obligation. Upon reflection he is truly sorry for what he said, candidly confesses his fault, and says that were he again placed in similar circumstances, he would not be guilty of the same fault. But suppose he should be asked whether, if the same degree of inattention, and the same envious feeling should again exist which characterized the state of his mind when he spoke unadvisedly, and no considerations should occur which were not then present to his mind, he is of opinion that he would act differently from what he did. Under such a view of the matter, few persons dare profess that they would act differently when placed in precisely the same circumstances. When we feel that we would and could act differently from what we have done in certain specified circumstances, it is always on the supposition that our views and feelings should be different. If the person speaking disrespectfully of a friend is asked what would induce him to act differently, if the thing were to be done again, the natural and reasonable answer is, "I

Example.

should think of the impropriety of the thing, and should recollect my obligations to the person; and other the like considerations." This shows that men feel accountable, not only for their volitions and actions, but for the views and feelings which precede volition. Indeed if there is one point above all others on which responsibility rests, it is on the motives, that is, the active desires or affections of the mind from which volition proceeds, and by which it is governed. The murderer could easily abstain from murder, if he would repress his malignant feelings; but with the same spirit of malice and revenge which induced him to shed his brother's blood, and with the same absence of all other views and feelings than those which he had at the time, there is a moral certainty that he would commit the same crime again. Nor has this certainty, that unrestrained malice and revenge would again lead to the perpetration of the same horrid crime, the slightest tendency to alleviate the guilt of the murderer. The true ground of his culpability, lies in his having and indulging such malignant tempers, and in voluntarily turning away his mind from all considerations of piety and humanity, which would restrain him from the cruel act. And here a question might arise respecting a man's desires and affections, and the power which he has over them; but this is not the proper place for a discussion of that point.

Another objection which has been repeatedly urged, and which by many is considered unanswerable, is, that according to this hypothesis, when two things exactly equal, and viewed to be so, are presented to the choice of a rational being, it would be impossible to choose either. But every man (say the objectors) feels that he has the power, if two loaves of bread or two eggs exactly alike be presented, of choosing between them; and as there exists confessedly no motive for preferring one loaf or one egg to the other, therefore it is possible for the will to determine without a motive.

Objection from impossibility of choosing between equals.

To this plausible objection it may be answered, that if the self-determining power of the will, independent of motives, be confined to

a

cases in which there are no motives to turn the balance, it is a power of very little

Answer.

importance, and not worth disputing about. Let it be admitted that in such an equipoise of motives, the mind can determine in favour of either of the objects. But perhaps this will admit of a different solution, and one in accordance with the theory maintained. And let it be remarked, that it is not the similarity of external objects which should here be considered, but the view which the mind takes of them. We know how a fertile imagination may cast a grain into one of the balanced scales, and cause it to preponderate. But further, the state of mind supposed to be produced by objects of equal value, is really felt for a moment. Between two things we hesitate, not being able to come to a decision; but this indecision arises not from a belief that the objects proposed are equal, but from a doubt which is preferable. When we are sure there is no difference, this hesitation is not experienced. The explanation which seems correct, is the following: two guineas are laid before a poor man, and he is told to take which one he pleases. It cannot be necessary that he should think one better than the other. If such a preference were necessary, he would be unable to take either, and his situation would be comparable to the ass of the old Greek sophists, held immovable between two bundles of hay.

The difficulty supposed to exist in the case of two equal objects proposed for our choice, is perfectly imaginary: no difficulty or perplexity is ever experienced, when the things presented to our choice are known to be equal. It is only when we apprehend that there may be a difference between the objects offered, that we hesitate. As if a person should offer to our choice two caskets, the contents of which are unknown; we find it difficult to choose, for the very reason that we suspect the one to be more valuable than the other, but are ignorant to which the greatest value attaches. And if we should be informed that one contained jewels of great price and the other nothing but baubles, our hesitancy would be accompanied with solicitude. But when we are certain that the things pro-

The difficulty unknown in fact.

posed to our choice are perfectly alike, in all respects, we experience no difficulty whatever. Suppose it to be first a single guinea which is offered to a needy beggar; he is moved by his feeling of want to take it. If instead of one, two guineas are offered, he experiences no difficulty in choosing, knowing them to be alike. But this furnishes no example of an action produced without a motive. The question is, whether the man shall act or not; and the motive for action is strong, namely, the desire of relief. As he is at liberty to take but one, and there is no difference between them, he seizes that, which from one or more of a thousand slight reasons of nearness or convenience, it happens to him to choose, without any preference properly so called.

CHAPTER XVIII.

SUMMARY VIEW OF LIBERTY.

Man intuitively certain that he is free.

MAN is conscious of liberty, and nothing can add to the certainty which he has that he is a free agent. Objections to self-evident principles, however plausible, should not be regarded; for, in the nature of things, no reasonings can overthrow plain intuitive truths, as no reasonings can be founded on principles more certain. Though we may not be able to understand or explain with precision wherein freedom consists, yet this ignorance of its nature should not disturb our minds. We experience the same difficulty in regard to other truths of this class without any diminution of our assurance. I am conscious that I have life—but what is life? neither I nor any other human being can tell. But do we, because of this ignorance, doubt whether indeed we live? Not in the least. We know that we are free precisely in the same manner that we know that we are living beings, and no plausible reasonings should disturb us in the one case more than in the other.

This certainty undisturbed by errors of reasoning.

Again, if in attempting to explain what is essential to free agency, we should fall into any mistake, or conclude that something does not belong to it, which does, let it not be said that we deny the freedom of man; for while we may err in regard to our conception of its nature, we know that we cannot err in regard to the actual existence of freedom.

Reason for denying some demands.

We are willing to attribute to man every kind and degree of liberty which can properly belong to a dependent creature and a rational being; and if we deny what some think essential to free agency, it is because in our view it would be no real privilege to possess such a power, as not being compatible with the laws by which rational creatures are governed.

It is admitted that man has power to govern his own volitions, and does govern them, according to his own desire. He has the liberty, within the limits of his power, to act as he pleases; and greater liberty, in our judgment, is inconceivable.

Postulates.

To suppose, in addition to this, a power to act independently of all reasons and motives, would be to confer on him a power for the exercise of which he could never be accountable. It would be a faculty which would completely disqualify him from being the subject of moral government. In the nature of things, it would be impossible that a creature possessed of such a power could be so governed that his actions could be directed to any end.

Liberty is not power to act independently of all reasons.

One hypothesis makes man the master of his own actions, but a creature governed by understanding and choice. He may be misled by false appearances, and influenced by wrong motives, but is always governed by some reasons or motives.

First hypothesis.

On the other hypothesis a man may and does act without any inducement, and without being influenced by any reasons, to do what is contrary to all his inclinations and feeling. I cannot but think that, after all, the abettors of this scheme retain in their minds a certain obscure but lingering persuasion that the free agent feels some reason for acting as he does; and if so, the dispute is at an end, for whatever may be the consideration which induces a man to act in opposition to strong desires, it must be something which is felt by the mind to have force, and to be such a consideration as ought to influence a rational being.

Second hypothesis.

Let us for still further elucidation again suppose a case in which this self-determining power is exerted.

A young man entrusted with the property of his employer, has by undue indulgence in amusements, contracted debts which he is unable to pay. He sees a way by which he can appropriate to his own use some of the

Case supposed for self-determining power.

money in his hands without the possibility of discovery. His wants are urgent, his reputation is at stake, and he feels himself impelled by a powerful motive to the deed; and there are no motives to draw him in an opposite course but such as are derived from conscience and the fear of God. At the moment when about to perpetrate the felonious act, he pauses and resolves that he will not do it. The question is, has he not power to act thus? Is he not the arbiter of his own acts of will? Are we not all conscious that we possess such a power? There is no dispute about the power, if it only pleases the agent to exercise it. He is as free to abstain from embezzling what belongs to another, as to do it. The only question is, will he do it unless some reason, motive, or moral feeling influence him? If so, then indeed it would be the exemplification of the power in question. But when we examine the case carefully we shall be satisfied that where there is a powerful motive on one side, there must be a preponderating motive on the other to prevent a volition in accordance with the first. Suppose the young man under the temptation mentioned to have his mind free from all moral considerations, and to have no fear of injuring his reputation, what would restrain him? Or, if without any moral influence, or any other consideration, he should abstain, would there be any virtue in the act? To know whether an act is virtuous, we properly ask, why was it done? what was the motive of the agent? But here there is none, and consequently the act can have no moral character. And if we suppose some faint remonstrance of conscience, and some slight fear of discovery, even these would not prevent the act where the contrary motives were urgent.

But suppose, now, this young man to have had a religious education, and to have been brought up to regard his reputation, and when the temptation is most powerful and he is in danger of yielding, conscience should utter her voice with power, and dictate imperatively that this is a deed which should not be done; and at the same time, a lively apprehension of disgrace should operate with a combined influence on his mind, would the operation of these motives in preventing the crime be less rational or less virtuous than if he should act without a motive?

CHAPTER XIX.

THE KIND OF INDIFFERENCE WHICH HAS BEEN CONSIDERED ESSENTIAL TO FREE AGENCY.

Acts of choice are free.

In every act of choice or will, it is implied that the person willing might, if he pleased, act in a different way from what he does, for otherwise he would be under a necessity of acting in one way only, and there could be no freedom in such an action. There is no freedom in the pulsations of the heart, for they are not voluntary, but go on whether we will it or not. In all actions where the will is exercised there must be at least two things which may be done. This liberty was by the ancients distinguished into two kinds, the liberty of *contradiction*, and the liberty of *contrariety*. In the first we have the choice

Liberty of contradiction and of contrariety.

of doing or not doing some proposed act. In the second, we have the liberty to do one thing or another, or one thing or several others. In regard to such objects of choice, there was said to be indifference, by which it was not meant that the mind was indifferent at the moment of choice. This would be a contradiction, because indifference towards an object, and the choice of an object, are opposite and irreconcilable states of mind. But the meaning was, that, abstractly from the feelings of the agent, the contrary or different actions were indifferent. It was in the power of the agent, *if he were disposed*, to do or not do, to do this or that; but it was never understood to imply, that with the inclination in one direction a choice might be made in the opposite direction. A man may do what he pleases, but it is absurd to suppose that he can will to do what it does not please him to do.

Power of contrary choice.

The doctrine of a power of contrary choice, as the thing has been now explained, is a reasonable doctrine, and in accordance with all experience, if with the volition you include the motive, if with the choice you take in the desire.

Volition cannot contravene prevalent inclination.

But to suppose a volition contrary to the prevailing inclination is inconsistent with all experience; and, as has been shown, such a liberty or power would disqualify a man for being an accountable moral agent.

Theory of Abp. King.

In the last century an able metaphysical writer, convinced that the common doctrine of the self-determining power of the will could not stand, invented a new hypothesis. His leading idea is, that we do not choose an object because we desire it, but desire it because we choose it. According to this view of Archbishop King, in his work on the "Origin of Evil," there must be a state of absolute indifference prior to an act of choice; for all love or attachment to an object, and all desire of possessing it, are produced by the act of the mind in choosing it. This is a complete inversion in the order of the exercises of the mind. Though recommended by high authority, and ingeniously defended by its author, it seems strange that it should have found any respectable abettors. But Dr. Watts, in his Essay on the "Freedom of the will in God and the creatures," adopts the outlines of the Archbishop's scheme, and defends its principles by many arguments. This led President Edwards, in his celebrated work on the Will, to take particular pains to refute this false theory. The indifference of which he treats is that which appertains to this scheme. Many, however, have been led, from an acquaintance with the work of Edwards, to suppose that the doctrine of indifference, as refuted by this great man, is common to all who maintain the opinion of the self-determining power of the will; which is far from being the case.

Adopted by Watts.

Refuted by Edwards.

It is deemed unnecessary to give a refutation of this theory in this place. Those who wish to see this effectually done may consult the several sections of the work of Edwards, to which reference has been made.*

* Edwards's Works, ed. New-York, 1844. Vol. ii. pp. 17-39. Part i., §§ 1-7.

CHAPTER XX.

WHETHER MEN ARE ACCOUNTABLE FOR THEIR MOTIVES; OR WHETHER DESIRES AND AFFECTIONS WHICH PRECEDE VOLITION, HAVE A MORAL CHARACTER.

Maxims which seem conflicting.

THERE are two maxims on this point, which we must endeavour to reconcile, as there is an apparent repugnance between them.

1. The motive gives character to the act. 2. The act is voluntary.

The first is, that every action takes its character from the motive from which it proceeds. The second is, that every moral act is voluntary, and therefore, that desires and feelings which precede volition, cannot be of a moral nature. This difficulty seems to have perplexed the perspicacious mind of Dr. Chalmers; for, perceiving that our desires and affections do possess a moral character, he labours, through a number

Chalmers.

of pages, to prove that, in as far as they are such, they are influenced by the will. The truth, however, is, that many of them are uninfluenced by preceding volition, and the whole reasoning of the learned author is unsatisfactory. The true solution is to be found in the ambiguity of language. When it is asserted that all moral actions are voluntary, the meaning is, either that by actions only external actions are meant, or that under the word voluntary, the affections of the mind which precede volition are included. No act of the body can take place without an action of the will preceding it; so that the maxim is true, as it relates to external acts. But it is also true in relation to mental acts, if we give a certain degree of extension to the word "voluntary," that is, if we use it as synonymous with spontaneous. Our desires are as free and spontaneous as our volitions, and when it is said that every moral act must be voluntary, the word is used in this comprehensive sense. There is no need, therefore, to prove that our affections must have received their complexion from a preceding volition. The judgment of the moral faculty in regard to the moral character of the desires and affections, is as clear and undoubted as of the volitions. Nay, the volitions receive their moral character from the quality of the motives which produce them; so that the very same volition may be good or bad, according to the moral character of the motives by which it is produced. The volition requisite in order to pull a trigger and let off a gun, is the same, let the motive be what it may. It is a determination to perform that specific act, and if it be performed by an insane person, there will be no morality in the volition. If the same volition be put forth by a person acting in his just defence, the volition and ensuing act will be good; but if the volition to shoot a man, arise from malice or avarice, the volition prompting the act will be wicked.

We must go higher than volition.

We do not, therefore, trace actions to their true moral source when we ascertain the volition from which they proceed; we must always go one step higher, and ascertain the motives.

When an investigation is made into the character of an act of which some one is accused, the main point, which by witnesses the court and jury wish to ascertain, is, from what motives the accused acted. Accordingly as this is determined, so is he judged to be innocent or guilty. It hence appears, that the true and ultimate source of the morality of actions, is not found in the will, but in the desires and affections. The simple act of volition, namely, a determination to do a certain act, is always the same, whatever be the motive. And to ascertain that an action proceeds from an act of will, only determines that it is the act of a particular agent, but gives us no knowledge respecting the true moral quality of the act. This will be found universally true. Two men are seen giving money to the poor; the acts are the same, and the volitions preceding the acts and prompting them, are the same; and as we cannot see the heart, we naturally judge that both acts are alike good. But if it should be revealed to us, that one of the persons was influenced entirely by a love for

Motives must be sought.

the praise of men, and the other, by a sincere regard for the welfare of the poor, we should immediately make a wide difference between the acts, in our moral judgment. We should still be convinced, however, that the volitions leading to the acts were the same, the only difference being in the motives.

Man accountable for his motives.

It is clear then that men are more accountable for their motives than for any thing else; and that, primarily, morality consists in the motives; that, is the affections.

CHAPTER XXI.

THE DIVISION OF MOTIVES, INTO RATIONAL AND ANIMAL.

Dr. Thomas Reid, in his work on the Active Powers, endeavours to maintain his doctrine that the will is not always governed by motives, by a reference to a certain distinction. Animal motives act by a blind impulse on the will, without regard to remote consequences. Rational motives operate by the force of reasonable considerations. Dr. Reid asserts that these classes of motives are so widely different, that their influence can never be compared: that what may be the strongest of one class, may be the weakest of the other, and that the mind must determine between them.

Reid's distinction.

The distinction is no doubt just. There are

principles in the human constitution, which act on the will with great force, by a blind impulse. Such are the appetites and passions, and the desire of happiness, and especially the desire to escape pungent pain, at present experienced.

The difference real.

The appetite of hunger urges the subject of it to eat, whether it can be done lawfully and consistently with health, or not. This influence is sensibly present, and it requires some strength of purpose to resist it, when the agent is convinced that the act cannot be done with propriety. Here then is the simultaneous operation of an animal and a rational motive; and it is evident that they counteract each other, and that according to the strength of one or the other, the will is determined this way or that way. It is not true, therefore, that these different kinds f motives cannot be compared as to their effective force. The fact is, they are brought into comparison every day, and every day victories are obtained by one over the other, according to the strength or influence which they re-

Appetite.

Whether the two can be compared.

spectively possess, at the moment. Hunger impels a man to eat; reason tells him that it will be injurious to health. Here is a fair trial of strength between the force of blind appetite, and rational regard for health. If the appetite be very strong, it will require a strong resolution to oppose it. In such cases, however, appetite commonly prevails; but not without resistance. In every case of the kind, there is a trial of strength between these different motives. Suppose food to be placed before a hungry man; if there be no considerations of duty or utility to prevent, he will of course indulge his appetite. But if he should be informed that the food is poisoned, although he be still impelled by his appetite to eat, yet the love of life or fear of death, will be sufficient to induce him to refrain.

Case of hunger and self-preservation.

Suppose, again, that the food is the property of another, whose consent to use it cannot be obtained. Here the moral feelings stand in the way of indulgence; and upon the comparative strength of his appetite and of the vigour of his

Case of hunger and duty.

conscience, will depend his determination. So far is it from being true, then, that animal and rational motives cannot be compared, in regard to their influence on the will, that there is nothing in human life more common than the experience of the struggle for mastery between the higher and lower principles of our nature.

The determination accords with prevalent desires.

When it is said that the mind determines between these contending motives, it is true, but not in the sense intended. It is true that the mind determines, and of course the volition is on one side or the other; but this determination is not independent of the strength of the contending motives, being always in accordance with the strongest existing desires.

The difference of the two.

There is this important difference between animal and rational motives, that a sensible impulse of the former as merely felt, is not of a moral nature. The hunger of a man is no more moral than the hunger of a beast. These animal feelings are unavoidable and constitutional. The point at which such feelings begin to partake of a moral quality, is when they require to be governed and directed. It was not wrong for the hungry man when he saw bread before him to desire it. But when he knew it to be the property of another, it would have been wrong to take it; and when he knew that the food would injure him, it became his duty to forbear.

We cannot extinguish the animal feelings by an act of the will; they arise involuntarily, and therefore cannot be in themselves of a moral nature. Yet as man has other principles and powers by which he should be governed, he becomes faulty when he neglects to govern these lower propensities in accordance with the dictates of reason and conscience. But in regard to other desires and affections, they are good or bad in every degree in which they exist. For example, not only are malice and envy sinful when ripened into act, but the smallest conceivable exercise of such feelings is evil; and as they increase in strength, their moral evil increases. It does not require an act of volition, consenting to these feelings, to render them evil;

their very essence is evil, and is condemned by the moral sense of mankind.

Concupiscence.

A clear understanding of this distinction might have prevented or reconciled an old dispute, viz. whether concupiscence* was of the nature of sin, in the first rising of desire, prior to any act of the will.

* It may remove ambiguity to say that the word *concupiscence* is here used not in its popular and modern, but its theological acceptation. The controversy to which allusion is made began early in the schools, and was actively waged at the time of the Reformation. The following references will enable the reader to inquire further: *Augustini*, Opp. x., ed. Benedict. pp. 387, 1029, 1828, 1881, 1955.—*Catechismus Conc. Trident.* ed. Lips. 1851, pp. 385, 386.—*Chemnitii* Examen. ed. Genev., 1641, pp. 88, 89, 90, 94, 95.—*Turrettini Instt.* P. ii. Qu. 21.—*Bretschneider*, Syst. Entwickelung; 4 ed. 1841, pp. 540, 541.

CHAPTER XXII.

WHETHER MORALITY BELONGS TO PRINCIPLES AS WELL AS ACTS, OR IS CONFINED TO ACTS ALONE.

Moral principles prior to volition.

It seems to be generally agreed, that in the human soul there exist certain principles from which actions proceed, as streams from a fountain; and that the character of the actions corresponds with that of the principle. Those, however, who maintain that the will possesses a self-determining power, independent of motives, deny the existence of any such principles lying back of the acts of the mind, especially in moral exercises. They hold that the evil of an act arises entirely from the exercise of free will, and that there is no propriety in referring it to any thing previously existing in the mind. They allege that nothing can be of a moral nature but that which is voluntary, and therefore that virtue or vice can be predicated of nothing but actions. They argue, however, that to make virtue and vice consist in the occult qualities of the soul, is to conceive of the essence of the soul as corrupt; and that this would be to make sin a physical quality, existing without any relation to the will. It would be entirely out of place, here, to consider the bearing of this controversy on certain theological points, concerning which polemics have waged an interminable war. We have, at present, nothing to do with any principles or questions but such as may be learned from reason and experience.

In the first place, let it be observed, that we know nothing of the soul but by its acts. We have no consciousness of any thing but acts of different kinds; yet we know as certainly that we have a soul, as that we think and feel. So, also, we are not conscious of the existence of what is called disposition, temper, principle; but we as intuitively believe in the existence of these, as in the existence of the soul itself. If

Principles argued from effects.

we see one man doing evil whenever he has the temptation, and another as habitually doing good, we cannot help considering that the one is actuated by an evil disposition which dwells in him, and that the other is influenced by a good disposition.

Whether moral good and evil may with propriety be predicated of these hidden tempers of the mind, must be determined by an appeal to the common judgment of mankind; and this, I think, is manifestly in favour of the affirmative. When a man is observed to manifest wicked, malignant passions as often as occasion serves to elicit them, all men agree that he possesses a malignant temper. The soul of such a man, when his acts of iniquity are finished, cannot be free from every taint, until he again put forth a voluntary act. The doctrine of a uniform series of evil acts, is irreconcilable with the doctrine that all evil consists in self-determined acts, unless the will itself be corrupt, for why should all acts be of one kind, when no cause exists why they should be one thing rather than another? We might suppose such a power would act as fre-

Morality predicable of principles.

quently one way as another. But if there be any causes without the will, which give a uniform character to its acts, then the will cannot be free. It is determined by something without itself, which is incompatible with the hypothesis.

Again: the fountain must partake of the quality of the streams. If these are uniformly evil, it is fair to conclude that the fountain is polluted. Voluntary wickedness is nothing else but bringing into act what before existed in principle in the soul. If malice in act is sinful, surely malice in principle must be evil.

Moral evil predicable of principles.

No man can bring himself to believe that the wretch who has perpetrated thousands of base crimes, and stands ready to commit others of the same kind, has no evil inherent in his soul, by which he is distinguised from the most innocent person.

Crime infers a bad principle.

Another evidence that men do judge something to be sinful besides sinful acts, is that men who palpably omit important duty, are considered equally guilty with those who offend by positive act. That man who neglects to rescue from death a human being, when it is easily in his power to do so, is by all men reckoned guilty of a great crime, though he performs no act of any kind. Suppose a helpless woman or infant to fall overboard from a boat, in which there is a strong man who might afford relief, but makes no attempt to do so. Is there a person in the world who would not view such a neglect as a great sin? Now, on what principle do we censure the person who has committed no act of transgression? Evidently on the ground that he ought to have felt a regard for the life of a fellow-creature. We blame his indifference to the welfare of his neighbour.

Proof from omission of duty.

As to the maxim, that nothing is sinful which is not voluntary, it relates to positive acts, not to dispositions of the mind. But as was explained before in regard to desires and affections, so in regard to dispositions, we say they are in a sense voluntary. They properly belong to the will, taking the word in a large sense. In judging of the morality of voluntary

Disposition, in what sense voluntary.

acts, the principle from which they proceed is always included in our view, and comes in for its full share of the blame. Thus Bishop Butler, in his excellent essay on the "Nature of Virtue," says, in speaking of the moral faculty, "It ought to be observed that the object of this faculty is actions, comprehending under that name active or practical principles." This sagacious man saw that it would not do to confine virtue to positive acts, but that principles must come in for their full share of approbation or disapprobation.

Proof from character.

The character which a man acquires by a series of acts, is not merely the estimation of a person who has performed such acts, but it is of a person possessing dispositions or principles which gave rise to such acts. Our notion of a bad man is of one who not only has perpetrated wicked acts, but is still disposed to do the same; and we disapprove the principle as much as the acts. The notion that corrupt principles must vitiate the essence of the soul, is without foundation. The soul is the subject of many affections which are not essential to it. Natural affections may be extirpated, and yet the soul remain unchanged. Moral qualities may be entirely changed, without any change in the essence of the soul. The faculties remain, while the moral principles which govern them may be changed from good to bad, or from bad to good. The same faculties which are employed in the performance of virtuous actions, may be occupied as instruments of wickedness. That inherent moral qualities may exist in the soul, has been the belief of all nations, and is the sentiment of every common man whose judgment has not been warped by false philosophy.

Common judgment of mankind.

Who can believe that the soul of a cruel murderer, whose heart cherishes habitual hatred and revenge towards his fellow-creatures, is, when asleep, or occupied with indifferent matters, in the same state of purity or exemption from evil, as the soul of the most virtuous man in the world? It cannot be believed. We cannot help thinking, when we see a uniform course of action whether it be good or bad, that there must be corresponding dispositions which lead to such actions. Every effect must have an adequate cause. Let it be granted, for the sake of argument, that the self-determining power is an adequate cause for any single act of any kind; yet it can be no sufficient cause for a series of acts of the same kind. This, however, must be left to the intuitive belief of every man. It is a subject for the judgment of common sense, rather than reason.

CHAPTER XXIII.

MORAL HABITS.

HABITS differ from principles, or constitutional desires, in that they are adventitious. Every habit is acquired by repeated acts.

The human constitution possesses a wonderful susceptibility of forming habits of every kind. Indeed, we cannot prevent the formation of habits of some kind or other. Still, a man has much in his power as it regards the kind of habits which he forms, and is highly accountable for the exercise of this power. A man's happiness and usefulness depend very much on the character of his habits. Yea, a man's moral character derives its complexion, in a great degree, from his habits. In this place, it is not necessary to go into the philosophy of the formation of habits. Habits.

Our object is to consider habits and habitual actions as they partake of a moral character, or as they are the object of moral approbation, or disapprobation. If we should remove from the list of moral actions all those which are prompted by habit, we should cut off the larger number of those which men have agreed in judging to be of a moral nature.

Accountability for habits.

That there are virtuous habits and vicious habits, will scarcely be denied by any considerate person. A habit of lying, of swearing, of slandering, of cheating; of irreverence, of indolence, of vainglory, with many others, are, alas, too common. There are also virtuous habits, such as of industry, temperance, kindness, veracity, diligence, honesty, &c. To be sure, these virtues commonly flow from principle, but the practice of them is greatly facilitated by correct habits. Two considerations will show that men are properly accountable for those actions which proceed from habit. The first is, that in the formation of his habits, man is voluntary. The acts by which they are formed are free acts, and the agent is responsible for all their consequences. The other consideration is, that habits may be counteracted and even changed by the force of virtuous resolutions and perseverance. Where habit has become inveterate, it may be difficult to oppose or eradicate it; but the strength of moral principle has often been found sufficient to counteract the most confirmed habits. When it is asserted that men long enslaved by evil habits cannot make a change, it is on the ground, that no principle of sufficient power exists in the mind of the agent; but for that deficiency, the man is responsible. Yet a power from without may introduce a new principle potent enough, to overcome evil habits. The importance of possessing good habits, is admitted by all moralists. Aristotle makes the essence of virtue to consist in "practical habits, voluntary in their origin," and agreeable to right reason. Dr. Thomas Reid, in his "Essay on the Active Powers," defines virtue to be "the fixed purpose to act according to a sense of duty," which definition Dugald Stewart modifies, by observing, "It is the fixed purpose to do what is right, which evidently constitutes what we call a *virtuous disposition*. But it appears to me that virtue, considered as an attribute of character, is more properly defined by the *habit* which the fixed purpose gradually forms than by the fixed purpose itself." Dr. Paley lays it down as an aphorism, that "mankind act more from habit than reflection." "We are," says he, "for the most part, determined at once, and by an impulse which has the effect and energy of a pre-established habit." To the objection, "If we are in so great a degree passive under our habits, where is the exercise of virtue, or the guilt of vice?" he answers, "in the *forming* and *contracting* of these habits." "And hence," says he, "results a rule of considerable importance, viz, that many things are to be done and abstained from, solely for the sake of habit."

CHAPTER XXIV.

THE NATURE OF VIRTUE.

THE theories on this subject have been numerous, and contrary to one another. It is now proposed to mention some of the principal of them. We shall first mention the theory of Mr. Hobbes and his followers, who deny that there is any natural distinction between virtue and vice, and maintain that by nature all actions are indifferent, and that our ideas and feelings on the subject of morality are altogether the effect of education and association. Mr. Hobbes did indeed maintain that men are bound to obey the civil government under which they may happen to live, and to conform to the religion established by

Various theories.

Hobbes.

Law of the land.

law, however contrary to their own private judgment. All moral duty, according to this theory, was resolved into the authority of the law of the land. As no natural moral rule existed, it was held that, except so far as a man was restrained by civil authority, he had a right to do what he pleased; and while he confined himself within these bounds, he need feel no concern about the consequences of his conduct.

Mandeville.

The defect of the hypothesis.

Epicurus.

Perhaps the most extraordinary system of virtue ever promulgated was that of Mandeville, who maintained that all pretensions to virtue were mere hypocrisy, which men assumed from the love of praise. This writer forgot that hypocrisy assumes it as true that that which is counterfeited is an object of esteem and approbation among men. That virtue consists in the mere pursuit of pleasure, or of our own interest, is a system as old as Epicurus, and has had many abettors up to this time. The arguments in favour of this theory are exhibited in their most plausible dress by Nettleton in his "Treatise on Virtue."

But the whole plausibility of the arguments depends on the pre-established connexion between happiness and a virtuous course of life. That true happiness is the natural effect of virtue, falls entirely short of proof that the essence of virtue consists in the tendency of certain actions to the person's true interest; whereas, when we perceive an action to be virtuous, we are conscious that it is not from any view of the connexion of the action with our own happiness that we approve it; but our judgment is immediate, founded on a moral character perceived in the act itself. And in many cases virtue requires us to deny ourselves personal gratification for the sake of others. A man supremely governed by a regard to his own interest, is never esteemed a virtuous man by the impartial judgment of mankind. According to this theory, the only thing censurable in the greatest crimes is, that the guilty person has mistaken the best method of promoting his own happiness. Upon this prin-

The Happiness theory considered.

ciple a man is at liberty to pursue his own interest at the expense of the happiness of thousands, and if he is persuaded that any action will tend to his own interest, he is at liberty to do it, whatever may be the consequences to others.

Archdeacon Paley.

Dr. Paley adopts the principle that all virtue consists in a regard to our own happiness, taking into view the whole of our existence. His definition is, however, a very complicated one, and deserves to be analyzed.

Paley's definition of virtue.

"Virtue," says he, "is the doing good to mankind, in obedience to the will of God, for the sake of everlasting happiness," according to which definition the good of mankind is the object, the will of God the rule, and everlasting happiness the motive of human virtue. If the question be asked, why we should seek the good of mankind, the answer is, from a regard to our everlasting happiness; and if the question be, why we should make the will of God the rule of our conduct, the answer must be the same;

so that really all virtue is resolved into a regard to our own happiness.

Now every man desires to promote his own happiness, and according to Dr. Paley's theory, the only difference between an eminently good man and one of the opposite character is, that the one pursues a wiser course than the other; but they are both actuated by the same motives.

Consequent difference between good and a bad man.

This theory loses sight of all intrinsic difference between moral good and evil, and admits the principle that happiness is the only conceivable good, and that any thing is virtuous the tendency of which is to promote our greatest happiness.

Neglects intrinsic moral differences.

A theory the opposite of that which makes a regard to private interest the ground of virtue, is the one which makes all virtue to consist in a regard to the public good. This is the theory of Bishop Cumberland in his work, *De Legibus*, and is not essentially different from the scheme of those

Cumberland.

who make all virtue to consist in disinterested benevolence. No doubt, much that deserves the name of virtue consists in good will to others, and in contributing to their welfare; but it is not correct to confine all virtuous actions to the exercise of benevolence. We can conceive of benevolence in a being who has no moral constitution. Something of this kind is observable in brute animals, and atheists may exercise benevolence to their friends. The indiscriminate exercise of benevolence to creatures, without any respect to their moral character, might appear to be an amiable attribute, but it could not properly be called a moral attribute.

Disinterested benevolence.

Regard for one's own welfare.

A prudent regard to our own welfare and happiness is undoubtedly a virtue. It has been considered so by the wisest of men, and we know that prudence was one of the four cardinal virtues of the heathen. As the whole is made up of parts, it is evident that if it is a virtue to promote the well-being of the whole, it must be so of each of the parts. The pursuit of our own happiness where it does not infringe on the rights of others, has nothing evil in it, but is approved by every impartial mind. Some who maintain that all virtue consists in benevolence, admit that we may seek our own happiness just as we seek that of our neighbour; but the human constitution is not formed to exercise that abstract impartiality. While we are bound to promote the welfare of our neighbour and of strangers, our obligation is still stronger to endeavour to secure our own happiness; and if a friend and a stranger stand in equal need of a benefit which we have it in our power to bestow, it is evidently our duty to consult first the welfare of our friend, other things being equal.

Abstract impartiality not to be expected.

What Bishop Butler has said on this subject in his short treatise on "Virtue," is worthy of consideration: "It deserves to be considered whether men are more at liberty, in point of morals, to make themselves miserable without reason, than to make others so; or dissolutely to neglect their own greater good for the sake of a present lesser gratification, than they are to neglect the good

Butler's remarks on the disinterested scheme.

of others whom nature has committed to their care. It should seem that a due concern about our own interest or happiness, and a reasonable endeavour to secure and promote it, is, I think, very much the meaning of the word *prudence* in our language—it should seem that this is virtue, and the contrary behaviour faulty and blamable; since in the calmest way of reflection, we approve of the first and condemn the other conduct, both in ourselves and others. This approbation and disapprobation are altogether different from mere desires of our own and their happiness, and from sorrow in missing it."

Benevolence not the whole of virtue.

Again, "Without inquiring how far and in what sense virtue is resolvable into benevolence, and vice into the want of it, it may be proper to observe that benevolence and the want of it, singly considered, are in no sort the whole of virtue and vice. For if this were the case, in the review of one's own character, or that of others, our moral understanding and moral sense would be indifferent to every thing but the degrees in which benevolence prevailed, and the degrees in which it was wanting. That is, we should neither approve of benevolence to some persons rather than others, nor disapprove injustice and falsehood, upon any other account, than merely as an overbalance of happiness was foreseen likely to be produced by the first, and misery by the second. But now, on the contrary, suppose two men competitors for any thing whatever, which would be of equal advantage to each of them, though nothing indeed would be more impertinent than for a stranger to busy himself to get one of them preferred to the other, yet such endeavour would be virtue, in behalf of a friend or benefactor, abstracted from all consideration of distant consequences; as that examples of gratitude and friendship, would be of general good to the world. Again, suppose one man should by fraud or violence take from another the fruit of his labour, with intent to give it to a third, who, he thought, would have as much pleasure from it as would balance the pleasure which the first possessor would have had in the enjoyment and his vexation in the loss; suppose that no bad consequences would follow, yet such an action would surely be vicious. Nay further, were treachery, violence and injustice, no otherwise vicious than as foreseen likely to produce an overbalance of misery to society, then, if in any case, a man could procure to himself as great advantage by an act of injustice as the whole foreseen inconvenience likely to be brought upon others by it would amount to, such a piece of injustice would not be faulty or vicious at all." "The fact then appears to be, that we are constituted so as to condemn falsehood, unprovoked violence, and injustice, and to approve of benevolence to some rather than others, abstracted from all consideration of which conduct is likely to produce an overbalance of happiness or misery."

Defective definitions of virtue are dangerous.

The danger of this theory is not by any means so great as that of the selfish scheme, because it comprehends a large part of actions which are truly virtuous. But all definitions of virtue which are not so comprehensive as to embrace the whole of moral excellence, are injurious; not only by leaving out of the catalogue of virtues such actions as properly belong to it, but by leaving men to form wrong conceptions of what is right and wrong, by applying a general rule, which is not correct, to practical cases. When it is received as a maxim that all virtue consists in seeking the happiness of the whole, and when a particular act seems to have that tendency, men are in danger of overlooking those moral distinctions by which our duty should be regulated. This effect has been observed in persons much given to theorize upon the general good as the end to be aimed at in all actions.

President Edwards has a treatise on Virtue, in which he enters very deeply into speculation on the principles of moral conduct. His definition of virtue has surprised all his admirers: it is, "the love of being as such." When, however, this strange definition comes to be explained, by himself and his followers, it amounts to the same as that which we have been considering, which makes all virtue to consist in disinterested benevolence.

Edwards on Virtue.

Dr. Samuel Hopkins, who was his pupil, and

well understood his principles, gives this as his definition of virtue, and has it as a radical principle of his whole system. It will not therefore be necessary to make any distinct remarks on President Edwards's theory.

Hopkins.

CHAPTER XIV.

THE NATURE OF VIRTUE, CONTINUED. DIFFERENT HYPOTHESES.

Aristotle's idea of the nature of virtue was that it was a mean between two extremes. Virtue, according to him, consisted in the moderate and just exercise of all the affections and passions; and vice, in defect or excess. It would be easy to show that this definition or description is not complete. It is not sufficiently comprehensive, and includes many things not of a moral nature. But it is unnecessary to dwell on the subject, as the definition is no longer used.

Aristotle.

Dr. Samuel Clarke, who has a long established character as a profound thinker, attempted to give a theory of virtue, which should be free from ex-

Clarke.

ception. He makes virtue to consist in acting according to the fitness of things. Whatever is fit and suitable to be done, taking in all circumstances, is right. But really, this gives us no conception of that peculiarity which renders an action virtuous. It is true, all virtuous actions are fit to be done, and are actions suitable to the circumstances of the agent. But every fit action is not a virtuous action, and the fitness of many actions depends on their moral character. Their fitness, therefore, does not render them virtuous, but their being virtuous is the very thing which renders them fit.

Wollaston.

Wollaston, in his "Religion of Nature Delineated," refines upon this system, and makes all virtue to consist in a conformity to truth. A virtuous action is one in accordance with the truth of things; which when it comes to be explained, amounts to much the same as Dr. Clarke's "fitness of things." Both of them include, no doubt, all virtuous actions, as they are all fit, and all in accordance with truth; but these definitions do not lead us to a conception of that quality in actions which is *moral.* Certainly all virtuous actions must be in accordance with truth and reason, but this is no definition of the nature of virtue; it is only a circuitous method of saying that some actions are virtuous because they have a fitness to produce a good end. This theory supposes the idea of virtue already to exist; for if the end be not good, mere *fitness* cannot be of the nature of virtue. There are other things which have a fitness to produce certain ends, as well as virtue. It is not mere fitness which renders an action virtuous, but adaptedness to a good end. And unless by truth we understand the same as virtue, it does not appear that a mere conformity to truth gives any conception of a moral quality, and there is as much reality in a vicious action as in one that is virtuous. On this subject Dr. Thomas Brown well observes, "Reason, then, as distinguishing the conformity or unconformity of actions with the fitness of things, or the moral truth or falsehood of actions, is not the principle from which we derive our moral sentiments. These very sentiments, on the contrary, are necessary, before we can feel that moral fitness or moral truth, according to which we are said to estimate actions as right or wrong. All actions, virtuous and vicious, have a tendency or fitness of one sort or other; and every action which the benevolent or malevolent perform, with a view to a certain end, may alike have a fitness for producing that end. There is not an action, then, which may not be in conformity with the fitness of things; and if the feelings of exclusive approbation and disapprobation, that constitute our moral emotions, be not presupposed, in spite of the thousand fitnesses which reason may have shown us, all actions must be morally indifferent. They are not thus indifferent because the ends to which reason shows certain actions to be suitable, are ends which we have previously felt to be worthy of our moral choice; and we are virtuous in conforming our actions to these ends, not because our actions have a physical relation to the end, as the wheels and pulleys of a machine have to the motion which is to result from them; but because the desire of producing this very end, has a relation, which has been previously felt, to our moral emotion. The moral truth, in like manner, which reason is said to show us, consists in the agreement of our actions with a certain frame of mind which nature has previously distinguished to us as virtuous, without which previous distinction, the actions of the most ferocious tyrant, and of the most generous and intrepid patriot, would be equally true, as alike indicative of the real nature of the oppressor of a nation, and of the assertor and guardian of its rights." The fitness and the truth, then, in every case, presuppose virtue as an object of moral sentiment.

Adam Smith.

The system of Dr. Adam Smith, contained in his "Theory of Moral Sentiments," is very plausible, as stated by its ingenious author, and has captivated many minds, by leading them to believe that the origin of our moral feelings is to be found in the principle of sympathy. According to this able writer, we do not feel the approbation or disapprobation, immediately on the contemplation of virtuous or vicious actions. It is necessary first to go through another process, by which we enter into the feelings of the agent, and of those to whom the actions are related, in their consequences, beneficial or injurious. If, on considering all the circumstances in which the agent was placed, we feel a complete sympathy with the feelings by which he was actuated, and with the gratitude or resentment of him who was the object of the action, we approve of the action as right; or disapprove it as wrong, if our sympathies are of the opposite kind. Our sense of the propriety of the action depends on our sympathy with the agent, and our sense of the merit of the agent, on our sympathy with the object of the action. In sympathizing with the gratitude of others, we regard the agent as worthy of reward; in sympathizing with the resentment of others, we regard him as worthy of punishment. When we judge of our own conduct, the foregoing process is in some measure reversed; or rather, by a process still more refined, we imagine others sympathizing with us, and sympathize with their sympathy. We consider how our conduct would appear to an impartial spectator; we approve of it if we feel that he would approve; we disapprove it if we think that he would disapprove. According to Dr. Smith, we are able to form a judgment as to our own conduct, because we have previously judged of the moral conduct of others; that is, have sympathized with the feelings of others. And but for the supposed presence of some impartial spectator, as a mirror to represent us to ourselves, we should as little have known the beauty or deformity of our own moral character, as we should have known the beauty or ugliness of our own features without some mirror to reflect them to our eye.

The hypothesis fanciful.

That a principle so irregular and capricious as that of sympathy should be made the origin of all our moral distinctions and feelings, is indeed wonderful. One might be tempted to suspect that the gifted author intended to select a subject merely for the display of his ingenuity in framing and defending a plausible hypothesis, and playing on the credulity of his readers.

The great error of this hypothesis is one which is common to most others on this subject: it takes for granted the existence of those moral feelings which are supposed to flow from sympathy—yea, their existence previous to that very sympathy in which they are said to originate.

Untenable.

When we suppose this previous moral feeling, it is easy to understand how we are led to approve of actions when we feel sympathy with the agent; but the most complete sympathy of feeling is not sufficient to account for the existence of moral approbation or disapprobation. When there is nothing more than a sympathy of feelings, without the previous moral sentiment, no such exercise as that which Dr. Smith supposes could ever arise; so that the process which he describes as originating our moral sentiments, never could take place, unless there existed previously a moral feeling in the mind. In contemplating the beauties of nature or art, we may have a complete feeling of sympathy with another person, our feelings may be in the most exact accordance, and yet no moral approbation of his sentiment of the beautiful be experienced. But if mere agreement in our emotions would

Assumes what is sought to be explained.

give rise to moral feeling, it ought to arise vividly in this case, where the emotions may be strong and in perfect accordance. "Why is it," says Dr. Brown, "that we regard emotions which do not harmonize with our own, not merely as unlike to ours, but as morally improper? It must surely be because we regard our emotions which differ from them as proper. And if we regard our own emotions as proper before we can judge the emotions which do not harmonize with them to be improper on that account, what influence can the supposed sympathy and comparison have had in giving birth to that moral sentiment which preceded the comparison? The sympathy, therefore, on which the feeling of propriety is said to depend, assumes the previous belief of that very propriety. Or, if there be no previous belief of the moral suitableness of our own emotions, there can be no reason from the mere dissonance of other emotions with ours to regard these dissonant emotions as morally unsuitable in the circumstances in which they have arisen."

The theory of Dr. Smith not only includes

the sympathy which we feel with the agent of an action, but also with the feelings of gratitude or resentment in the object of the action, as it may affect others with benefit or injury. If we feel that in similar circumstances our emotions would sympathize with theirs, we regard the agent in the same light in which they regard him as worthy of regard in one case, and of punishment in the other; that is, as having moral merit or demerit. It is evident that this is an inadequate and defective account of merit and demerit; for it confines these qualities to actions which relate to the welfare of others; but all impartial men judge that actions of a different kind may have merit or demerit. If a man, from a sincere desire of improvement in virtue, is led to deny himself habitually such gratification of his senses and appetites as would interfere with his progress, and to submit to a course of discipline to overcome evil habits, which is both difficult and painful, and yet perseveres in the midst of numerous temptations to relax, until he has obtained a complete victory over himself; who

Inadequate and defective.

would say that there is nothing in all this to call forth moral approbation? But the actions have no respect to the happiness of others; there is no gratitude or resentment with which the observer can sympathize.

Theory of conformity to the will of God.

That theory which considers conformity to the will of God to be virtue, is undoubtedly correct; for that faculty in us which approves of virtuous actions was implanted by Him, and is an induction of his will. As soon as we get the idea of a God we cannot but feel that it is the duty of all creatures to be conformed to his will. But if the question be whether, in judging an action to be virtuous, it is necessary to consider distinctly of its conformity to the will of God, we are of opinion that this conception is not necessary to enable us to perceive that certain actions are morally good and others morally evil. In order to this judgment nothing is required but a knowledge of the circumstances and motives of the action. Even the atheist cannot avoid the conviction that particular actions are praiseworthy, and others deserving blame. But though belief in the existence of God is not necessary to the exercise of the moral faculty, yet this belief adds great force to the dictates of conscience, and enables us to account for the existence of a faculty by which we discern qualities so opposite in the actions of moral agents. Indeed, to know that our conduct should be conformed to the will of God, supposes the existence of a moral faculty, of which this is one of the intuitive judgments. If we had no moral faculty, the obligation to be conformed to the will of God would not be felt.

Dictates of conscience strengthened by Theism.

But intuitive moral perceptions have not this basis.

It is true, undoubtedly, that it may be inferred from clear data, that ultimately all duty and all virtuous actions may be referred to the will of God as the standard by which they should be tried. Our original intuitive perception of the moral character of certain actions does not, however, take in this idea, but is an immediate judgment of the mind upon observing such actions. Morality is a quality seen in the actions themselves.

If the question be asked, why we should be conformed to the will of God? the answer is, because it is right,—morally right. We must then have a faculty of judging respecting moral obligation before we can know and feel that conformity to the will of God is right.

Morality is presupposed.

CHAPTER XXVI.

THE NATURE OF VIRTUE. CONTINUED.

VIRTUE is a peculiar quality of certain actions of a moral agent, which quality is perceived by the moral faculty with which every man is endued; and the perception of which is accompanied by an emotion which is distinct from all other emotions, and is called moral. This quality being of a nature perfectly simple, does not admit of being logically defined, any more than the colour of the grass, the taste of honey, the odour of a rose, or the melody of tune.

Virtue.

As some actions are morally good, which are virtuous; so there are other actions which are morally evil, or vicious. The perception of these, also, is accom-

Vice.

panied by a feeling of a moral kind, but very different from that which accompanies the view of virtuous actions.

The judgment immediate.

Virtue, then, may be said to be that quality in certain actions which is perceived by a rational mind to be good; and vice, or sin, is that which a well-constituted and well-informed mind sees to be evil. Whatever may be the rule or standard of virtuous actions, the immediate judgment of the moral faculty on contemplating the act is necessary. Without a moral faculty we never could have the least idea of a moral quality, good or bad; therefore all actions must be brought before this faculty, and its judgment is ultimate. We can go no further. While the good or evil of some actions is self-evident, much discrimination and reasoning are requisite to arrive at a clear view of the true moral character of others. But the end of these processes is to bring the true nature of the action in question fairly before the mind, when it is judged by the moral

The moral faculty necessary.

faculty. Those actions, then, which a sound and well-informed mind judges to be morally good, are virtuous, and those which such a mind judges or feels to be evil, are sinful.

As has already been explained when treating of conscience, the judgment of the mind respecting moral qualities, is the judgment of the understanding, and differs from other judgments only by the subject under consideration. The mind must possess the faculty of moral perception, of which all the inferior animals are destitute. To see that an action is useful, and will produce happiness to him that performs it, or to others, is one thing; but to perceive that it is morally good, is quite a distinct idea; and virtue and mere utility should never be confounded. It may be thought that this account of virtue makes the moral faculty the only standard of moral excellence. In one sense, this is true. It is impossible for us to judge any action to be virtuous, which does not approve itself when fairly contemplated by our moral sense. To suppose otherwise, would be to think that we

The moral judgment is peculiar.

and some other faculty by which to judge of moral actions than the moral faculty. As no judgment of colours can be formed but by the eye, nor of sounds but by the ear, nor of odours and tastes but by the senses of smelling and tasting; so no judgment can be formed on moral subjects, but by the moral faculty. It may be asked, then, whether the judgments of this faculty are infallible, and if so, how it is that we have so many discrepant opinions, respecting the morality of actions. To which it may be answered, that when the mind is in a sound state, and any moral action is presented to it, with all the circumstances which belong to it, the judgment of this faculty is always correct and uniform in all men. As an eye in a sound state judges infallibly of colours, in which judgment all in precisely the same circumstances will agree in their perceptions; so it is in regard to moral qualities. If in looking at an object, one man has more light than another, or if one occupies a more favourable point of observation, the object will appear differently to the persons thus situated;

Whether infallible.

but this does not argue that their eyes are differently constructed, or that there is any other faculty than the eye, by which the object may be surveyed. So, in regard to moral qualities, when they are presented to different minds with precisely the same evidence, the moral judgment will be the same. The differences observable in the dictates of the consciences of men, may be all traced to some cause which prevents the object from being perceived in its true light; such as ignorance, error, or prejudice. In regard to sin and duty, the ultimate appeal must be to conscience. We may bring considerations of various kinds to bear on the conscience, or to enlighten the mind, so that the moral faculty may be rightly guided; but still our ultimate rule must be the judgments of our own moral faculty.

Discrepant judgments, whence.

And here it may be remarked, that conscience will recognise every new relation into which a moral agent enters, and will dictate the obligation to perform the duties obviously arising out

New relations occasion views of new duties.

of such relations. Or, if such an agent should for a time be ignorant of its relations, and afterwards discover them, it would, upon such discovery, feel an obligation not before experienced. Let us then suppose the case of a child educated in a cave, who, while the intellectual powers were cultivated, and the faculties developed, had never been informed respecting the existence of its parents and the relation it sustains to them. Of course, while in this state of ignorance, there would be no sense of obligation to them; but so soon as the nature of this relation should be clearly made known, the obligation to the obvious duties arising out of this relation, would immediately be felt. Let it be supposed, also, that this human being, until grown to maturity, had never heard of God, and of course possessed no idea of such a being. While in that state of ignorance, it could have no sense of the obligation to reverence, love and serve its Creator; but as soon as the mind should take in distinctly, the conception of God as the Author of its being, and as possessed of every adorable attribute, the

Duty of a creature as such.

duties arising out of this newly-discovered relation, would be felt to be obligatory. A just consideration of this relation would lead to the conclusion that, in every thing, the will of such a Being, standing in such a relation to the creature, should be obeyed. Thus the important principle would be learned, that the will of God, so far as made known by reason or revelation, should be the supreme rule of moral conduct. Conscience, henceforth, would act under the influence of this truth. And making the will of God—so far as made known—the supreme and only rule of moral conduct, would not be found at all inconsistent with the obligation to obey the dictates of conscience; for it would now become evident that God, being the author of our minds, had constituted them with this moral faculty, to admonish them of duty, so that the dictates of an enlightened conscience are the clear indications of the law or will of God. It is the law written on the hearts of all men.

The will of God seen to be obligatory.

Nothing can be considered as partaking of

the nature of virtue which does not meet with the approbation of the moral faculty. This will by some be thought a dangerous principle, merely from a misapprehension of its nature. They allege that the will of God is the only perfect and immutable standard of moral rectitude. They allege, moreover, that to define virtue to be only such actions as the moral faculty in man approves, is to make it a very uncertain and fluctuating thing, depending on the variable and discrepant moral feelings of men.

Virtue predicable only of objects of moral approbation.

This objection confounds two things which should be kept distinct, viz., the quality of an object and the light or medium through which it is viewed. The colour of an object can be perceived only by the eye; but in order to have the object fairly before the eye, there must be light reflected from it, and that light on entering the pupil, must be reflected so as to be conveyed to a focus on the retina. But without an eye it would be useless to descant ever so long or so learnedly on the nature of colours, or the laws

Answer to objection.

by which light is reflected and refracted. In the case of sight, it is evident that all the perception which is experienced, must be by the eye. If the light is insufficient, it must be increased, and if any cause hinders it from being duly refracted, vision will not take place; but still, it is only by the eye that we can have any perception of colours.

Analogy of taste.

Perhaps an illustration, drawn from the faculty of taste, may be more appropriate. A beautiful landscape is presented; I am charmed with its beauty. This emotion or feeling of the beautiful depends on the faculty of taste. If that were absent, I might see all the objects as they stand, and perceive nothing of the beautiful. Beauty in the works of nature or art can be perceived only by taste, and the emotion will depend on the perfection of the faculty, provided the object is presented in a favourable light. A person of cultivated taste sees beauties where a rude savage sees none. Thus also in regard to moral acts, or a connected series of moral actions, every idea and feeling of a moral kind must as necessarily be through the moral faculty as colours through the organ of vision. We have no other faculty which takes cognizance of moral qualities. The judgments and emotions which are produced by the contemplation of such actions, are always infallibly correct, when the mind is duly enlightened and the faculty itself in a sound and healthy state. There is no inconsistency between this opinion and that which considers the will of God as the real standard and ultimate rule of moral conduct.

Moral feelings dependent on the dictates of understanding.

For, as has been shown, although conscience can act within a narrow sphere without even the knowledge or belief of a God; yet so soon as this knowledge is obtained, and the mind recognises its relation to its Creator, a new field is opened for the operations of conscience. It is soon perceived that the clear dictates of conscience, in cases of self-evident truth, are nothing else than the indication of the law of God written on the heart of every man, as was before taught. We can refer to the will of God as a rule of moral conduct no other way than by the exercise of the moral faculty, by which it is clearly perceived that our Creator and Preserver has a just claim on our obedience, and ought in all things to be obeyed. But if conscience did not thus dictate, all appeals to the will of God, to show what is morally right, would be in vain. The certainty and immutability of our moral standard of rectitude will then be in proportion to the knowledge which the mind possesses of the existence of God and the creature's relation to Him. Instead, therefore, of making our moral feelings mere instinctive emotions, as is done by Hutcheson and Shaftesbury, we make them depend on the clear dictates of the understanding; for, as we have often explained, the judgments of conscience are no other than the understanding judging on moral subjects.

Evil of attempting undue simplification.

If that, and that alone is virtue, which is approved by a mind duly enlightened, and in a sound state, then the attempt to reduce all virtuous actions to some one kind—as to benevolence, for example—is not the way to arrive at the truth.

For while benevolent actions generally meet with the approbation of the moral faculty, we can easily conceive of an exercise of benevolence which, instead of being approved, would be viewed as morally indifferent, or merely amiable—as a natural affection, or even as evil. We never ascribe morality to the kind feeling of brutes to one another. The natural affection of parents, called *storge* by the Greeks, is no more of a moral nature than the same affection in inferior animals. The natural affection of our relatives, our neighbours, and countrymen, is amiable and useful, but not of a moral character. If a judge should feel a strong benevolence toward all criminals, so as to avoid inflicting on them the penalty of the wholesome laws of the country, we should judge it wicked. It might be said that a benevolence which counteracts a greater good, is not virtuous but sinful; yet it is an exercise of benevolence, and serves, on the concession of those who make all virtue to consist in benevolence, to show that all benevolence is not virtue, which is the very thing to be proved. Again, there are acts of moral agents, which have nothing of the nature of benevolence, yet which the moral faculty judges to be morally good. For example, if a man for the sake of moral improvement, denies himself some gratification which would in itself be pleasing to nature, we judge such self-denial to be virtuous.

Prudence a Virtue.

A thousand acts of prudence which have regard to our own best interests, without interfering with the interest of others, have always been reckoned virtuous. Indeed, among the ancient sages, prudence was one of the four cardinal virtues. The attempt, therefore, to reduce all virtue to the simple exercise of benevolence, must be unsuccessful. It is so evident that some actions which have our own welfare as their object, are virtuous, that rather than give up their theory that all virtue consists in benevolence, they enlarge the meaning of the word, so as to make it include a due regard to our own welfare. But this is really to acknowledge that all virtue does not consist in benevolence, according to the usual meaning of that word. Any term may be made to stand for the whole of virtue, if you choose to impose an arbitrary meaning upon it. Benevolent affections, however, is a phrase which has as fixed and definite a meaning as any in the language, and by all good writers is used for good will to others. Benevolent affections are, therefore, constantly distinguished from such as are selfish. If, however, any one chooses, contrary to universal usage, to employ the words in a sense so comprehensive as to include self-love, be it so. We will not dispute with such a one, about the meaning of the word, provided he agree that the judicious pursuit of our own improvement and happiness is virtuous.

Actions to be classified.

To determine how many different kinds of actions are virtuous, we must pass them in review before the moral faculty, and then classify them; being in the whole process governed by the light of true knowledge, and taking into view all the relations in which the human race, or any portion of it, is placed. Something of this kind we may attempt in the sequel of this work, in which we shall endeavour to survey the moral duties incumbent on men, in their various relations.

CHAPTER XXVII.

WHETHER VIRTUE AND VICE BELONG ONLY TO ACTIONS.

Moral acts are complex.

It has repeatedly been brought into view that moral qualities are found only in actions of moral agents, and not in all actions, but only in those performed under certain circumstances. But when we consider those actions which are of a moral nature, we find that they are complex, consisting of an external and internal part. At once we can determine that a mere external or corporeal action can possess no morality, except as connected with the internal or mental exercise which produced it, and of which it is the exponent. But here again there are several acts of the mind clearly distinguishable from one another, and it is of importance to determine in which of these the moral quality exists. On this subject there is a diversity of opinion. It seems commonly to be taken for granted, that the act of volition is, so to speak, the responsible act, and this has led to the maxim almost universally current, that "no action is of a moral nature which is not voluntary."

Moral acts voluntary.

Accordingly, writers of great eminence have entertained the opinion, that to render our desires and affections moral, they must directly or indirectly proceed from volition. But here arises a serious difficulty. Our desires and affections are not subject to our volitions.

Desires not subject to volition.

We may will with all our energy to love an object now odious, and our will produces no manner of effect; except to show us our inability to change our affections by the force of the will. On the contrary, we find by constant experience that our volitions are influenced uniformly by our prevailing desires. No man ever put forth a volition which was not the effect of some desire, feeling, or inclination. Now, after the most attentive examination of our minds, we find that certain affections which are neither produced by volitions nor terminate in volitions, are, in the judgment of all reflecting men, of a moral nature. For example, envy at the prosperity of a neighbour is not the result of any volition, and it may be cherished inwardly without leading to any volition, the will being controlled by other feelings which prevent action; yet all must admit it to be a morally evil disposition. The truth then appears to be, that our affections are properly the subject of moral qualities, good and evil.

Yet desires have moral quality.

Volitions take their character entirely from the internal affections or desires from which they proceed. The volition, viewed abstractly, is always the same, when the external action is the same; but the moral character of the acts, where the volitions are the same, may vary exceedingly. If, I will to strike a man with a deadly weapon, the simple volition which precedes and is the immediate cause of the action, is the same whether I give the stroke in self-defence, in execution of the law, or through malice prepense. Indeed,

Whence volition has its quality.

the volition of an insane person to strike a blow is exactly similar to the volition of a sane person striking a similar blow. Hence it is evident that the proper seat of moral qualities is not i the will, considered as distinct from the affections, but in the affections themselves, which give character to the volition as much as to the external action. These internal affections or desires are properly the springs of our actions, and our wills are the executive power by which they are carried into effect. They are commonly called motives, and very properly, as they move us to action; but I have avoided the use of that word, because it is ambiguous, and has occasioned much misconception on this subject. By motives, many understand reasons or external qualities in the objects of our desires; that which excites or moves our affections. Then when it is asserted that the will is governed by the strongest motives, some understand the meaning to be the strongest reasons, or those qualities in an object best adapted to excite our

The true spring of actions.

Motives.

affections. In this sense the proposition is not true. Minds are often in such a state that they are not governed by that reason which in their own view is the strongest; that is, which in their better judgment seems wisest and best. And often our minds are not influenced or governed by those external objects or considerations which in the judgment of impartial reason are most weighty. But if by motives be understood the desires themselves, actually in exercise at the time, however produced, then it may be truly said that the will is always determined by the strongest motives, that is, the strongest desires. But even this proposition needs qualification. The strongest single desire does not always govern the man, but the strongest combination of desires, as may be thus exemplified. A man in returning from a journey on a cold day has a strong desire to reach home without delay; but passing a house where he knows he can enjoy a warm fire, and good refreshment, and the company of a friend, though

Whether governed by the strongest reasons.

In what sense will follows the strongest motives.

his desire to reach home is stronger than his desire to see his friend, stronger than his desire to enjoy the fire, or his desire for food or drink, yet all these combined prove sufficient to induce him to stop.

Morality of an act from its intention.

It is often said that the intention or end for which an action is performed, determines its moral character; and as our desires always point to some object which is the end of the action, this account of the matter coincides with the view already given. As if a man gives money to another, though we see the action, and are sure that it was voluntary, yet that determines nothing respecting the moral character of the action. Before we can judge any thing correctly, we must know the intention with which the act was performed. If it was to pay a just debt, we approve it as a moral act, but of small merit. If it was to supply the wants of a poor suffering family, unable to help themselves, we still approve, but our approbation is much stronger; the act is more meritorious than the former. But if we are informed that the person on whom the benefit was conferred was an enemy who had sought every opportunity to injure him who is now his benefactor, we esteem it the highest degree of Christian virtue. But if it should appear that the money was given to a common drunkard, to enable him to procure intoxicating drink; though the external act and volition are the same, instead of approving the action, we censure it as culpable. And finally, if it should appear that the intention was to hire an assassin to murder an innocent person, and that person a benefactor, our emotion rises to the highest degree, and we reprobate the action as evil in the extreme. In all these cases, the action and the volition producing it, are the same. The only difference is in the end or intention with which it was done. The intention will serve to characterize actions very well, but is not comprehensive enough to take in all the exercises of mind which possess a moral character. I feel habitually a kind disposition to my fellow-creatures, but for much of my time I have not the opportunity of performing any particular acts of kind-

The assertion qualified.

ness. All impartial persons will say that this habitual feeling is of a virtuous character; but there is no intention in the case. It is merely a feeling which terminates in no volition or action.

Intention not comprehensive enough.

My neighbour, who has been a bad man, undergoes a real change of character, and from being profane and quarrelsome, becomes pious and peaceable. I rejoice in the change. This joy is a virtuous emotion, though it has no intention accompanying it. This will serve to show that making the intention the sole characteristic of morality, is correct in regard to actions, but is not comprehensive enough to take in the whole of morality.

Objection.

It may seem that in what has been said, we contravene the maxim, that all moral actions are voluntary, a maxim which has received the sanction of ages, and may be considered an intuitive principle: whereas it is now maintained that there are exercises of mind which do not involve any exercise of will; and that our volitions themselves have nothing of a moral nature but what they derive from the motives from which they proceed.

The maxim, rightly understood, is no doubt just, and we should never affect the wisdom of being wiser than the common sense of mankind, where we meet with truths in which all men of sober reflection have been agreed. It is safer to take them for granted, as believing that universal consent in such matters furnishes the best evidence of truth.

The maxim admitted.

But the explanation is easy. The maxim applies primarily to *actions*, which must be voluntary to have the character of morality. If the action is not voluntary, it is not properly the action of the person who seems to perform it, for we can act in no other way than by the will.

The objection removed.

But again, the word *voluntary* as employed in the maxim under consideration, includes more than volition; it comprehends all the spontaneous exercises of the mind; that is, all its affections and emotions. Formerly all these were in-

Ambiguity of term *voluntary*.

cluded under the word *will*, and we still use language that requires this latitude in the construction of the term. Thus it would be consonant to the best usage to say that man is perfectly voluntary in loving his friend or hating his enemy; but by this is not meant that these affections are the effect of volition, but only that they are the free spontaneous exercises of the mind. That all virtue consists in volition, is not true—as we have seen; but that all virtuous exercises are spontaneous, is undoubtedly correct. Our moral character radically consists in our feelings and desires. These being the spontaneous actings of certain latent principles or dispositions, this hidden disposition is also judged to be morally evil, because it is productive of such fruit. And of good dispositions we judge in like manner.

Scholastic acceptation of *Will*.

CHAPTER XXVIII.

THE AUTHOR OF OUR BEING CONSIDERED IN RELATION TO MORAL SCIENCE.

Preceding truths lead to argument for a Supreme Being.

IT has already been intimated, that the very existence of conscience seems to indicate, that man has a Superior to whom he is amenable for his conduct. The feeling of moral obligation which accompanies every perception of right and wrong, seems to imply, that man is under law; for what is moral obligation but a moral law? And if we are under a law there must be a lawgiver, a moral governor, who has incorporated the elements of his law into our very constitution. This argument for the existence of God, is solid, and independent of all other arguments; and it goes further than arguments derived from the evidences of design, which abound in the world around us; for these prove no more than that the Author of our being is intelligent, but this argument proves that he is a moral Being, and exercises a moral government over us. The Atheist, when he feels, as he must, remorse for some great crime, can scarcely help believing, that there is a God who is displeased with his wicked conduct, and who will punish him hereafter; for the keen anguish of remorse seems to point to a punishment which is future. Hence it is that when Atheists come into those circumstances which have a tendency to awaken the conscience, they for the time become believers in the existence of God. Thus in a storm at sea, even the most confirmed Atheist has been found calling upon God, for deliverance; and when death is suddenly presented to them, they often find, that their atheistical theories cannot withstand the power of an awakened conscience. Certainly the existence of an accusing conscience cannot in any way be so well accounted for, as by the supposition that man is the creature of a Being who intended to form him in such a manner, that he should have a control over his actions, and who

Atheism practically recanted.

has left an indelible proof of his authority in the mind of every man.

But omitting to press this argument further at present, let us attend to some of the other evidences of the existence of a God. No one can contend that there is any thing absurd in the idea of an eternal, all-powerful, intelligent, First Cause, from whom all things have received their being. No one can doubt that the supposition of the existence of such a Being seems to account for the phenomena of nature; and it is equally certain, that they cannot be rationally accounted for on any other hypothesis.

Argument against Atheism.

To deny that in animals and vegetables there are evident marks of design, would be as unreasonable as to deny that any thing exists. Thus the eye was formed to see, the ear to hear, the mouth to masticate our food, the stomach to digest it, the various internal organs to separate the particles suited for nutrition from the mass, and by a wonderful and inexplicable process to convert, or assimilate these particles into the

Teleiological argument.

various forms and organs which constitute the human body. For any man to affirm that in all these contrivances and operations, there is no evidence of design, is certainly to contradict the intimate conviction of his own reason. It may on many accounts be expedient and highly profitable, to accumulate arguments from design, as manifested in the rational, animal, vegetable, and mineral world; but for mere argument and demonstration, these details are unnecessary. A man cast away on a desolate shore, would be as certain that some rational beings had been there, if he found one watch, or one quadrant, as if he should see a thousand of such like or other works of art, strewed along the shore. His mind is soon satisfied with the force of this evidence, as observed in a few particulars, and the conviction of the truth, that these things are the effect of a designing cause, is as perfect as it can be, by the contemplation of ever so many instances. It may, I think be taken for granted, and even Atheists will admit, that we cannot conceive of any works, or contrivances, which

A few instances of design sufficient.

would more clearly evince design, than those which are found in the human, and other animal bodies. Though it is said that some ancient Atheists attributed every thing to chance, yet it seems unnecessary to take up much time in combating such a theory. Atheists no longer resort to this very absurd notion. As then design manifest in any effect, leads necessarily to the conclusion, that intelligence exists in the cause; there is no escape from the conclusion, that the cause of the existence of animals and vegetables is a wise and powerful Being, but by one of the following suppositions. 1. That every thing in which design is manifest, has existed from eternity; or, 2. That there are in the material universe, causes possessing power and intelligence to produce these effects, but no one great intelligent person; or, 3. That there has existed from eternity a succession of these organized beings, producing one another in a continued series; so that while the individuals in the series perish, the succession is eternal.

Chance.

The first supposition is too extravagant, we

should think, to have any advocates. Indeed, as it relates to the bodies of animals and vegetables, we have a certain demonstration, that their organization has a beginning. And if every thing was from eternity, every thing would be immutable and imperishable; but we see every kind of organized bodies tending quickly to destruction. Our souls also had a beginning, for their gradual increase and development is a matter of daily observation. We have no remembrance of an eternal existence, nor any consciousness of independence, which must be an attendant of an eternal being. We are conscious that we cannot cease to be, nor control our own destiny. Nothing is more certain in the mind of all thinking men, than that we who now live are creatures of yesterday. But it is unnecessary to refute an error which perhaps no one is so unreasonable as to hold.

1. Eternity of the universe.

Let us then consider that atheistical, or rather pantheistical scheme, which attributes all the appearances of design in the world to the world itself; that is, to certain causes existing in the world which produce beings of various species, not by creation out of nothing, which they hold to be impossible, but by an evolution or development of principles contained in the world itself. According to this theory the world is God, and all things are parts of this one being.

2. The hypothesis of evolution.

This theory would avoid the name of Atheism, which has ever been odious; but it retains the virus of the poison of Atheism under another name. It admits a cause, or rather multitude of causes, capable of producing these marks of design; but denies that this cause, considered as one or many, is a person. The question necessary to be determined is, what is necessary to constitute a person? Here we have intelligence in the cause, in the highest conceivable degree. But the structure of the body of man is not mere intelligence; there is an adaptation of means to an end. This supposes the exercise of choice or selection, which is obviously an exercise of will. Every instance of contrivance therefore evinces

Denies a personal God.

Personality.

the exercise of an intellect and will; and that being in which these two properties are found, we are accustomed to denominate a person.

It would be difficult to find a better definition of a person. But we need not dispute about the name; when there is manifest evidence of wise contrivance in the effect, there must be an intelligent cause to produce such an effect. Where, we ask, is that cause? Is it in the individual which exhibits these signs of design? That would be to make the same thing cause and effect. Is there then for each individual in which wise contrivance appears a particular cause; or is nature or the world to be considered one general cause, operating in a multitude of ways? To suppose a particular cause for every one of these effects, would be to multiply deities beyond the wildest mythology of the heathen; for these causes being intelligent beings, possessing a wisdom beyond our conception, each is properly considered a separate deity. But even this supposition comes utterly short of furnishing a satisfactory account of the pheno-

A single cause demanded.

mena of the universe; for the admirable contrivances in the natural world consist very often in the adaptation of things which are entirely distinct, to each other, as of the light to the eye, the air to the ear and to the lungs, the food to the stomachs of the various species of animals, &c. The same adaptation is equally obvious in the vegetable world. That cause, therefore, which produced the eye must have produced the light; and the cause of the curiously-contrived apparatus of hearing must have formed the air; and the author of the stomach must have adapted it to various kinds of food, &c. The hypothesis of an infinite number of separate, intelligent causes, will not be maintained. All these effects must be attributed to one cause, and that cause must be infinitely wise and powerful, to give existence to so many wonderful works.

If, then, there is one cause of all these different species of beings, which could not exist without wise contrivance, that cause must be powerful, intelligent and benevolent; but power, wisdom, and intelligence can exist only in some being,

Attributes required in this sole Cause.

and that being which possesses them must be a person. The Pantheist will allege that these attributes belong to the universe itself, and therefore there is no need to suppose any being to exist separate from, and independent of the world. All these phenomena arising, are only the developments of this one substance, in which the attributes before mentioned have their seat.

The Pantheistic reply examined.

Before we receive such an opinion, let us inquire what constitutes the universe, as far as our knowledge can extend. We become acquainted with the world without us by our senses. Trusting to the information of these inlets of knowledge, we find that the universe consists, as far as known to the senses, of peculiar objects, combined together in various ways. These material things, though subject to peculiar laws, appear entirely destitute of intelligence. In this, all men agree. The light, the air, the water, the rocks, the earth, the metals, &c., are not capable of thought. Indeed, every material thing with which we are acquainted consists of an infinite number of parts, even when of the same kind, and no otherwise related to each other than that they are situated near to each other; whether they are at all in contact, we do not know. If thought belonged to matter, each of these infinitesimal particles of matter would be a conscious being, and his consciousness be independent of every other particle. By what medium of communication could these particles of matter agree on forming an organized body? But the Pantheist does not believe that matter is endued with thought. His theory is, that in the world there exists not only external substance, but thought or intelligence in the same substance. But as this intelligence must have a subject in which it resides, and of which it is a quality, and as it cannot be an attribute of brute matter, there must exist a substance distinct from matter, of which it is a property. Matter being divisible, inert, and extended, cannot have intelligence as an attribute, which is active, indivisible, and unextended. Extension, and thought, therefore, cannot be properties of the same substance. If then the cause of the phenomena of nature which indicate design is in the world itself, the world must, besides the gross matter which we see and feel, be possessed of a soul, or spiritual substance, in which this intelligence resides. This would bring us to the old Pagan theory of the *Soul of the World.* Under the material part, but under this only, there is a spiritual substance, a soul; just as in a man, we can see and feel the body, but we know that within this case, there exists a spiritual substance or soul. This theory, then, admits the existence of a great spirit, possessing the attributes necessary to account for all the appearances of wisdom in the world. It differs from the common theistical doctrine only in this, that it would confine this being to the world; but for this, there could be assigned no valid reason. A being possessing such power over matter as to mould it into every organized form found in animals, vegetables, and minerals, must have a complete control over matter, and be perfectly acquainted with all its most hidden properties and capabilities, and must be independent of matter, and must exist every where, to carry on the processes of nature. And as we do not know the extent of the material universe, we can set no limits to the presence of this spiritual, intelligent and omnipotent being. The object of Pantheism is to get clear of the idea of a personal God, who gives laws to creatures, and superintends and governs them according to their natures. But the hypothesis, if it could be established, does not answer the purpose for which it was devised. Still, even according to the hypothesis, we must have a personal God, who knows all things and rules over all.

3. Eternal succession.

The only other atheistical method of accounting for the phenomena of the world, as indicating the most consummate wisdom, as well as the most omnipotent power, is the hypothesis, that the universe in its present form has existed from eternity, and that all the various species of animals and vegetables now observed have always existed, and have communicated existence to one another in an endless series. And as an eternal series has no beginning, it can have no cause. There is therefore no need of supposing any first cause, from whom every thing has proceeded. As we must suppose some being to exist from eternity, we may as well suppose that the world which we see is that eternal being.

Fortress of Atheism.

This has always been the stronghold of atheism, and therefore deserves a more special attention. The only reason, however, which gives an advantage to this theory is, that it carries us back into the unfathomable depths of eternity, where our minds are confounded by the incomprehensibility of the subject. It is also to be regretted that some truly great men, in attempting to refute this theory, have adopted a mode of reasoning which is not satisfactory. This, we think, is true with respect to Bentley, who possessed a gigantic intellect; and, as might have been expected, many are his followers. Dr. Samuel Clarke has also pursued a course in his reasoning on this point, which, to say the least, is not entirely free from objection. The same may be said of many others, and especially of some who have attempted a mathematical demonstration of the falsehood of an infinite series of living organized beings, including the celebrated Stapfer.

It will be an object, therefore, to free the

subject as much as possible from intricacy and obscurity, and to present arguments which shall be level to any common capacity accustomed to attend to a train of reasoning. We may certainly assume it as an admitted principle, that every effect must have not only a cause, but an adequate cause. If wise contrivance and evident adaptation of means to an end be found in the effect, to ascribe it to an unintelligent cause, is as unsatisfactory as to assign no cause.

Argument against eternal series.

This then being assumed, we would take this position as incontrovertible, that if design manifest in one effect requires an intelligent cause, the same necessity requires the same kind of a cause for any number of similar effects; and the conclusion must be the same, whether the number is finite or infinite. This evident truth has been often and happily illustrated, by supposing a chain suspended before our eyes, but reaching beyond the sphere of our vision. The lowest link requires a support, and so does the second, and there is no less need of support

An adequate cause still indispensable.

for every successive link as you ascend the chain; and if you suppose as many links beyond your sight, as there are atoms in the universe, still the same necessity of a support is presumed to exist. There must ultimately be a support for all these suspended links. But suppose some one to allege that the chain is of infinite length, and has no beginning, we immediately begin to experience some confusion of ideas. We attempt to grasp infinity, and finding ourselves baffled in the attempt, we are apt to lose sight of the proper logical conclusion in this case. The necessity of a supporting power has no dependence on the number to be sustained. If one, if one hundred, if one thousand require support, so does any number of links. The conclusion is not in the smallest degree affected by the number, except that the more links, the stronger must be the supporting power; but this has nothing to do with our present argument. The conclusion will be of the same kind, and will as necessarily follow, in the case of effects which have in them the marks of design. The number cannot affect

No relief from making series of effects infinite.

the conclusion. If one such effect cannot exist without an intelligent contriver, an infinite number of great effects cannot. If multiplying one cipher, or zero, by any number in arithmetic, produces nothing, and the same is the result of multiplying a thousand ciphers, the conclusion is inevitable, that an infinite number of ciphers multiplied by any number cannot result in any positive quantity. Indeed, if all the individuals in the supposed infinite series are of the same kind, all are effects, and it is absurd to conceive of an effect without a cause. Cause and effect are correlative and imply each other; and if an effect cannot exist without a cause, much less can an infinite number of effects exist without an adequate cause.

Cause must be existing and operative.

My next argument will leave out of view altogether the idea of infinity, which is so apt to confound the mind. It is this. Every effect must not only have a cause, but that cause must be in existence and operation; for it would be absurd to think of a cause operating, when it no longer had an active existence. Let us then take that individual of a series of organized beings which came last into existence. Let it be an animal—a dog or horse. This individual we know came recently into being; when produced there must have been an adequate cause in existence and in operation. What was that cause? The hypothesis confines us to the preceding series of animals of the same species, supposed to have come down in uninterrupted succession from eternity. But whether the series be long or short, finite or infinite, is of no consequence as it relates to our present argument. What we are inquiring after is a cause in existence at the time this curiously organized and animated being came into existence. Now at that time, the individuals of the series had all ceased to exist, except the immediate progenitors. Whatever cause existed, cannot therefore be looked for in them; and if the effect is such as manifestly to be beyond any power and skill which they possessed, the contriving and efficient cause cannot be found in the series. There must be a higher cause.

But lest some persons should have a vague notion that some hidden power might be communicated through the series, although not found in the progenitors of the animal under consideration, I will lay down a principle which is admitted in mechanical powers, and is equally applicable to all causes. It is this. In all cases where any power is communicated through a series of individuals, the whole power necessary to produce the effect, must not only be communicated to the first, but to every single thing in the series, until it reach the last, which is intended to be affected by the original power. Thus, suppose it to be required to communicate motion to a ball in a plane, by sending an impulse through a hundred balls, the principle known to all mechanicians is, that the force necessary to give the desired motion must be communicated to the first, and from the first to the second, and so on, until it reaches the ball intended to be moved. And this principle is equally applicable to all causes which operate through a succession of particulars. If at the

The whole power of the cause must be carried through the series.

commencement of a series, an intelligent cause operated, and then ceased, or stopped short of the last effect, no sign of intelligence could exist in this, which brings us back to the same obvious principle with which we commenced, viz., that when any effect is produced, an adequate cause must exist, and be in operation at the time of its production. The simple inquiry then, is, had the progenitors of this dog, or horse, when the animal came into existence and became animated, the skill necessary to continue the animal frame, with all its curiously contrived parts, and power and skill to give to this individual that constitution of instincts, appetites, and passions suited to its condition in the world, which it possesses. I leave the atheist to answer this question? The same course of reasoning will be equally forcible as applied to fruits and vegetables. Every one of these organized beings furnishes an irrefragable argument for the being of a God; for in any one of these is evidence of the existence of a wisdom and power which certainly do not exist in the several particulars of which the series consists.

The only modern attempt to invalidate the argument for the being of God founded on the appearance of design in the universe, is that of Mr. Hume, which is substantially this, that this argument supposes that we have seen similar works performed, from which, by analogy, we conclude that an intelligent cause is necessary to account for them; as if we find a watch we believe it to have been made by an artist, because we have before observed such works made by skilful men; but in relation to the world, it is a singular work, entirely unique. We have never seen any world produced, and, therefore, the reasoning which would hold in regard to the conclusion that the watch was made by an artist does not apply.

The Atheistic objection of Hume

More importance has been given to this objection, especially by Dr. Chalmers, than it deserves. The objection of Hume is a mere sophism, and can unsettle no mind which understands the nature of the argument in question. According to Mr. Hume's argument we could not

Reply

infer from any work of art that it had an intelligent author, unless we had seen a work of the very same kind by an artist. Suppose a boy who has never been away from his father's farm, where he has seen nothing superior to ploughs, carts, and harrows, to be conducted to a seaport, and to see a steam-frigate. As he has never seen on the farm any thing formed like this, according to Mr. Hume, he could not infer that this stupendous work was produced by an intelligent cause. To the boy it would be a singular effect, the like of which he had never witnessed, and, therefore, he could infer nothing respecting it. Now every child knows better than this. Any boy of common sense will conclude in a moment that this steam engine must have been the work of a skilful artificer.

The world not a singular effect.

In order to apply the argument from design, it is not at all necessary that we should have seen an artist engaged in producing its like. All that is necessary is, that there should immediately appear an adaptation of means to produce a certain end; and it matters not as to the argument whether we ever conceived of a similar work, or knew any thing of the artist, the certain appearance of design, or a skilful adaptation of means to an end is always sufficient to produce the certain conclusion that there has been a designing cause at work. The works of nature are not a singular effect, as far as the argument a posteriori is concerned. The adaptation of means to an end in these is similar to the works of design among men. The difference between a telescope and the eye of an animal is not so great as between a plough and a steam engine. If there was any difference between the inference from seeing a steam-frigate or a complicated spinning engine, which have never been seen before, and another plough or cart, it would be in favour of the contrivance not before witnessed. The argument seems to be *a fortiori* in this case. And as the whole argument in regard to the works of man is founded simply on observing an adaptation of means to accomplish an end, and not the adaptation to produce some particular end which we had before seen effected by similar means; and as the adaptation of means to an end is as evident in the works of nature as in the works of man, the argument is as conclusive in one case as in the other.

CHAPTER XXIX.

THE PHENOMENA OF THE UNIVERSE.

LET us now suppose that a Great Intelligent First Cause exists, and has existed from eternity; are not all the appearances of the universe correspondent with the existence of such a being?

Accords with phenomena.

Again we may demand of an Atheist what other evidences of the existence of God he would require. Let him suggest something, which, in the form of evidence, would be more satisfactory to him, and he will not find it easy to fix on any evidence which is stronger or more suitable than what we already possess.

Unreasonable to ask more evidence.

It may appear strange to some that we challenge the Atheist to demand any clearer or stronger evidence of the existence of a Supreme Being than that which is already before us. But let the attempt be made to conceive of some evidence of this truth which would be more satisfactory, and better adapted to be a standing proof to all nations, and we have mistaken the matter, if the result will not be that the existing evidence is as good as any which they could ask. It will be worth while to spend a little time in considering this point, for if we cannot satisfy the Atheist of the truth of our position, the discussion may be satisfactory to others who have not been accustomed to view the subject in this light.

Atheist challenged to propose any stronger.

It is true we do not see God, and the reason is, he is a spirit; and a spirit, from the very nature of the case, is invisible. We cannot see the souls of our nearest friends; we know that they exist, not by any direct perception of the intelligent substance, but by the actions which they perform through the instrumentality of the body. If God were not a spirit he could not be an active,

Visibility of God not requisite.

intelligent, powerful, and perfect being; but being a spirit he must be invisible. Nothing is visible but material substances, and these only by means of light reflected from them to the eye.

Invisible existences are believed in.

It is not forgotten that most Atheists, being materialists, deny that there is any such substance as spirit; but they do not and cannot deny that there is something within us which thinks and feels and wills, and has power to originate bodily motion. Call the substance, of which thought is a property, by what name you please, still it is an invisible substance. Who can pretend to see a thought or a volition? or who would say that he can see the mind, and describe its shape and give its magnitude and dimensions? Let it be supposed then that the cause of all intelligence has a nature resembling this intelligent nature of which we are every moment conscious, but far more excellent, as it must be supposed that every excellence exists in a higher degree in the cause than in the effect.

Now supposing such an intelligent being to exist, call him spiritual or material, only let him be a being of thought, will, and passion; and that he is necessarily from his nature invisible to eyes of flesh; the question is, how could such a being make himself known to rational minds such as ours. As we cannot by any direct perception look into the mind of another, and as such a being cannot make himself visible without assuming a gross body, we can conceive of no way by which he can make himself known but by performing some act, or exhibiting to us some work which shall contain the impress of his character. For if he should assume a bodily shape, and thus make himself visible, it would not be the intelligent substance which we perceived, but a body, which was no part of his essence. If an intelligent creature could be so situated in the universe as to have no opportunity of contemplating any work of God, such a creature could never arrive at the knowledge of his existence. But the supposition is impossible; for an intelligent creature

In no way could spiritual Being be better revealed.

could not exist without the consciousness of its own thoughts; and in the mind itself, even if it were cut off from all perception of material things, there is sufficient proof of an efficient, intelligent cause. The impress of the divine attributes is as clearly printed on the soul as on any of the works of God to which man has access.

The First Cause known by his works.

As the First Cause, if there is one, must be from his nature invisible, the only way by which he can be conceived to make known his existence, is by setting before us some work, in which his wisdom, power, and goodness may be manifested; and by the contemplation of which a rational mind may infer, that a being does exist, to whom these properties belong. If then in the various objects in the world, there is as much evidence of these attributes as we can conceive, and in fact far exceeding our most enlarged conceptions, we have the best proof of the existence of a Great First Cause, which we couldhave. The simple question then is, could there be exhibited stronger evidences of wisdom than we have in the structure of the body of man, and in the constitution of his mind? Could the various species of animals in the earth, air, and sea, be formed with more consummate wisdom than they are, in relation to the climate in which they live, and the provision made internally and externally for their subsistence, and the propagation of their kind. Examine also the vegetable world. Call in the aid of glasses to inspect the concealed structure of the vessels; contemplate the leaf, the flower, and the mature fruit, and say whether you can conceive of contrivances more exquisite. If any man thinks that animal and vegetable bodies could have been constructed with more wisdom, let him point out in what respects these works of nature are deficient in wisdom. But even if it were possible to conceive of more perfect works, this could not in the least invalidate the argument from them, for he existence of an intelligent cause. If the question were of the degree of perfection in the wisdom exhibited, then the skill manifested in each work would be a proper subject for consideration. An imperfect time-piece proves the existence of an artist as fully as one that is perfect.

But there is here no need of this remark, for the Atheist may be defied to conceive of any improvement in any of the works of God, in regard to the adaptation of the means used to the end to be accomplished; and these evidences of the wisdom of God are scattered profusely over the whole universe. We cannot turn our eyes to the heaven or the earth, to objects of great magnitude, or so small that they can be seen only by the microscope, but the same admirable perfection of contrivance is manifest in them all. The internal structure of the gnat is as wonderful as that of the elephant; and in the manifestation of wisdom in the creation there is a wonderful variety. No two species are exactly alike; and the difference is exactly such as it should be to accomplish the special end in view. The more intricate our examination of the contrivance and evident design in the organization of animal and vegetable bodies, the stronger will

This manifestation needs no amendment.

be our conviction, and the greater our admiration.

The only question then is, could the evidences of intelligence in the cause, if thus innumerable, be exhibited in a clearer and stronger light than they are; if not, then God could not make known his existence as an intelligent being more clearly than he has done. The number of instances in which design appears, is far greater than can be examined, and the degree of wisdom in the various contrivances in organized bodies, transcends our conception; how, therefore, could we have by new works, greater evidence of an intelligent cause, than we already possess?

God is clearly manifested.

But there seems in most minds a lurking suspicion, that the existing evidence is not as convincing as it might have been. Even if this were so, we have no right to complain, when it cannot be denied that we have very strong evidence. God is not obliged to give to his creatures the strongest possible evidence of his

The evidence need not be as great as possible.

own existence. He may choose to leave scope for human industry, and also make the reception of the truth a part of our moral probation; and the pleasure of discovering truth after laborious research, a part of the reward of virtue. No doubt this is the fact in regard to some truths of no small importance. The honest inquirer discovers them, while the proud and prejudiced mind, though more acute, misses them, and embraces in their stead dangerous error. In maintaining, therefore, that the evidence for the being of God is as convincing as it could be to an impartial, rational mind, it is not because such clearness is considered essential; but simply because the fact appears to be as stated.

Can stronger proof be proposed?

But since many may still suppose that they can imagine much stronger proof than any which exists, let us consider what can be alleged in favour of this opinion.

Could not God speak to us in a voice of thunder, and thus make himself known? Undoubtedly he could; and such a voice would doubtless greatly terrify us; but would it be a stronger proof of his wisdom and power than the works of nature, which we behold? If this tremendous sound were heard very often, it would at length become familiar, and would cease to produce the same impression as at first. If heard but seldom, it would leave a suspicion that it might have been no more than a disordered imagination. But how could we be sure that the voice proceeded from a being who would not deceive? The mere hearing the noise could give us no certain evidence of the character and veracity of the speaker?

Supposition of address to the ear.

But perhaps it may be thought that a glorious visible appearance would place the matter beyond all possibility of doubt. The majestic appearance of a divine person, would, it may be alleged, satisfy every one. The same objections may be made to this species of evidence, as to the former; how could we know that this visible appearance was that of the Great First Cause? Unnatural appearances prove nothing

A visible glory not convincing.

respecting the character of the person who assumes them; if such apparitions were only occasionally exhibited, we should be prone to doubt of their reality; and if frequent, we should become too much accustomed to them to receive any impression. But whatever impression such appearances might make, considered as evidence of an all-perfect Deity, they would not be comparable to that which we have in the works of nature.

Miracles

But if the Supreme Being exists, why could he not make himself known by working stupendous miracles? Of course, if miracles might be demanded by one, all have the same need; and the same claims and miracles would become so common, that it would be difficult to distinguish them from natural events. And again, miracles require no more power to produce them than is required to produce common events. In many cases they would require no more than a cessation of the power by which natural events are produced. The standing still of the sun, or the stopping of the rotation of the earth, would be nothing else than removing the impulse by which they were originally put in motion.

Are effects of power

In a miracle, we only see the effect of divine power. We may infer from this, that there is a Being who can change the laws of nature; and a miracle taken by itself can prove nothing more. But in the works of nature, we have innumerable proofs of the wisdom and beneficence of the Author of the Universe. And the number, variety, and wisdom of these works are evident to every person of common sense. The proofs of a great intelligent cause are spread out, over the heavens and the earth, the sea, and the air. We are little affected by these objects, because they have ever been before our eyes since our earliest infancy. But as evidences of a Divine existence their force is not diminished by the uniformity of the laws of nature, by which they are continually produced, but greatly increased. The different species of animals and vegetables have successively been reproduced, according to laws that never vary; and this shows that the plan of the Almighty is perfect, and that He can accomplish all his pleasure, and has given uniform laws to every kind of being which his wisdom and power have produced.

It is not denied that miraculous displays are a decisive proof of a Great First Cause, who is possessed of omnipotence; but what we maintain is, that the evidence of omnipotence is not greater than in the natural effects which are constantly produced before our eyes. And as to the character and attributes of God, they are far more clearly exhibited in the various productions of nature, than they would be by a miraculous interposition. If another sun were placed in the heavens, which is as great a miracle as we can imagine, it would be a proof of mighty power, but not a stronger proof than the existence of the natural sun; and as to the wisdom and goodness of the Deity, there would be no comparison, for in the former case, nothing but the existence of Omnipotence could be inferred from the miracle, for there would be no appearance of wisdom in such a miracle. But in the existence of the natural sun, which gives light,

But add nothing to proof of power.

heat, motion, and life to all earthly living things, the wisdom and goodness of the Creator are most illustriously displayed. Who can enumerate the benefits which are derived from the influence of the sun? and the same sun, which communicates so many blessings to our world, dispenses blessings in the same way to other planets.

Result of the argument.

If we saw the dead raised in a thousand instances, it would be a decisive evidence of the existence of a Being of almighty power; but the evidence is fully as strong from the formation and vivification of innumerable animal bodies of many species. And no miracle can be conceived, which would furnish stronger evidence of the Divine existence, than the works of creation which are ever before our eyes and our minds. I think, after what has been said, that we cannot wish for more convincing evidence of the existence of a Supreme Being, than we already possess in the works of nature spread out before us; and even if we were shut up in a dark dungeon, we have this convincing evidence in our own persons, in the constitution of both our souls and bodies.

The demand of self-evidence.

The only thing which can be alleged further is, that this might have been made a self-evident truth as much as our own existence, or the existence of the world without us; and many formerly entertained that opinion that the idea of God is innate, and that a speculative Atheist is a thing impossible. Some very learned and respectable philosophers and theologians have expressly inculcated this opinion in their writings. Now, although we do not believe there are any innate ideas, and although the existence of God can scarcely be said to be self-evident, yet in the proof of it, there is but a single step of reasoning. It is a self-evident truth that every effect must have an adequate cause; and when there is evident design in the effect, the cause must be intelligent. The conclusion is so easily drawn from an intuitive truth, that it is not wonderful that it should be classed among self-evident truths. We can scarcely conceive of the state of that mind which after seriously contemplating the wonderful evidences of design in the human frame, can doubt the existence of an intelligent First Cause, and an intelligent cause producing effects by a wise adaptation of means to a definite end, and the harmonious operation of thousands of parts in the vital functions must, according to every proper definition of the term, be a person.

Attributes of God.

All the arguments by which the being of God is proved, involve the proof of some of his attributes. If the marks of design in creatures prove the existence of a Creator, it is by showing that he must be possessed of wisdom to cause so many wonderful contrivances as we behold in the world. As the operation of any cause is the exertion of power, so the creation of the world is the action of omnipotence. A greater power than that which brings something out of nothing cannot be conceived: this indeed we cannot comprehend, and, therefore, some who admit that the world is the work of God, as far as relates to the organization and moulding of matter, yet cannot be persuaded that omnipotence itself can give existence where there was none before. But if God did not create the matter that is in the world, whence came it? There are but two suppositions; one is, that matter existed from eternity, and is, therefore, self-existent and independent; the other, that it is an emanation of the divine essence. The first is inadmissible; it supposes two eternal beings independent of each other, and the latter leads to pantheism, or that all things are a part of God; as whatever emanates from him must be a part of his essence, for this is immutably the same. Though wisdom and power are the attributes which are first observed, they are not the only attributes of which we may learn something by studying the works of nature. For when we attentively consider the nature of the end, to accomplish which the innumerable contrivances are adapted, we cannot but observe that this end is beneficent. All the parts of animals are connected with the vitality, enjoyment, and preservation, of the animal or species. The goodness of God is therefore as manifest in the creation, as his wisdom. There is not a part in any animal body which can be shown to be without its use. Every species is fitted by the bodily structure, and by the instincts and passions with which it is endued, to enjoy in th most perfect degree that kind of life to which it is destined. Even the minutest animalculæ have bodies organized with as exquisite skill as those of the larger species. No living creature exists for which food is not provided, suited to the appetite and nourishment of the species, and which it has the means of procuring. So every species is endowed with the instinctive ability to provide for itself and its progeny suitable places of residence; and there are insects which, though they undergo a remarkable metamorphosis and change of appetites, are still able by their instinct to find the nourishment which is agreeable and necessary. And what is still more wonderful and indicative of far-seeing wisdom in the Creator is the fact, that these insects which were once in the chrysalis state, and afterwards assume the form and instincts of butterflies, are led by an invariable propensity to deposit their eggs on plants necessary for the young grubs, but on which they themselves never feed. Were it not for this wise provision for the young, they would all perish. Between the animal and vegetable world there is a beautiful harmony; the latter to a large extent supplies food for the former. It may be thought that the constitution of things by which one animal preys upon another, is an argument against the goodness of God; but these animals are only intended for a transitory existence, and as they all must die, and are tormented with no apprehensions in regard to the future, and the pain indeed is momentary, if they enjoy much more pleasure than pain during their existence, there seems to be no solid objection against this law of nature.

It has often been alleged as an atheistical objection against the goodness, and by consequence, against the existence of God, that pain or misery has a place among his works. This perhaps is the most plausible of all objections which infidels have ever produced; and yet it has no certain principles on which to rest. With a

Objections from existence of pain.

system such as the present, where there is a gradation of sensitive beings, it is impossible for us to conceive how all pain could be excluded. As far as we can see, the susceptibility of pleasure carries with it a liableness to some degree of pain. What if the pain which animals endure arise out of the principle of self-preservation, and from the appetites, in the gratification of which consists their enjoyment? Without desire and appetite there could be no animal enjoyment, and when the safety of the animal requires it, it is wisely ordered that by uneasiness or pain it should be stimulated to seek its necessary food, or flee from danger.

Miseries of the human race.

And as to man, while in the present world we cannot conceive how he could have any enjoyment, unless he was also subject to such feelings of uneasiness as rendered him capable of relishing his enjoyments. This remark relates to pains which cannot be avoided, such as the pain of hunger and thirst, and the pain arising from contact with some injurious body. The surface of man's body is the chief seat of pain, because danger commonly approaches him from without. It does not appear, therefore, possible that such a system of creatures as exist in the world could be constituted so as to be exempt from all uneasy feelings. To make creatures whose constitution would exempt them from all liableness to pain, would, as far as we can see, exempt them from all susceptibility to pleasure. And as to those evils which men bring upon themselves by imprudence, intemperance, injustice, or by disobeying the voice of conscience within them, they must be attributed to themselves and not to the constitution of the world. And as God is not obliged to make every creature as great and as happy as it could be made, it may seem to exhibit his wisdom and power to produce beings in whose existence there is a mixture of natural good and evil.

Moral perfections of the First Cause.

It appears clear, then, that the Author of this universe is powerful, wise, and beneficent; but how does it appear that he is possessed of a moral character? that he loves moral excellence, and disapproves of moral evil? This appears evidently from the moral constitution of man. The law interwoven in his constitution proves that his Maker approves of moral excellence. Again, it would be absurd to suppose that the creature could possess an excellence, and one superior to all natural endowments, of which there was no prototype in the Great First Cause. We may lay it down as a maxim, that whatever perfection we can conceive of must exist in the most perfect degree in the Creator, for all our ideas of perfection are derived from the contemplation of creation; and whatever excellence there is in the creation must exist in the Creator.

Divine approbation of virtue.

Besides, by the laws of nature, virtuous conduct is generally productive of pleasure and peace of mind; and immoral conduct is generally a source of misery. These laws of nature are the laws of God, and manifest his approbation of virtue and disapprobation of vice.

CHAPTER XXX.

DUTIES OF MAN TO THE CREATOR AS THUS MANIFESTED.

Foundation of law.

HAVING given, in a summary, the proofs of the existence and character of God, so far as reason can guide us in the inquiry, we are now prepared to consider the relation in which man stands to God, and the obligations which arise out of this relation. As man himself, in the wise and wonderful constitution of his mind and body, has been supplied with the most striking and convincing evidences of a powerful, wise, and beneficent Author of the universe; we are led at once to see, that God, as being the Creator of man, and the Giver of all his remarkable endowments, has a perfect right to claim his obedience, to the utmost extent of his powers. And on taking an impartial survey of the origin of his being, of the goodness of the Creator in his various beneficent endowments, and of his continual dependence, not only for the continuance of his being, faculties, and susceptibilities, but also for all those gifts of divine Providence necessary to his health and comfort, man cannot but feel that he is under the strongest moral obligation to obey, honour, and glorify his Maker, with his best affections and most strenuous exertions. This is the foundation of what is called the law; that moral law which is, as it were, written on the heart of every man; for what man is there, who has come to the exercise of reason, who does not perceive a clear distinction between right and wrong? And where can be found a human being, who, upon having his relation to God as his Creator set before him, does not feel in his conscience, that he is under a moral obligation to be subservient to his will?

General obligation.

The general obligation on all moral agents, to serve their Creator, is evident enough. It will require some time, and careful consideration of this relation in which man stands to his Maker, to ascertain the particular duties which are obligatory on all men.

Particular obligation.

This we shall now attempt, so far as reason can guide us in this matter.

Obedience internal.

Here it may be proper to remark, that the essence of all obedience is internal; that is, consists in the dispositions, affections, and purposes of the heart. Outward actions partake of a moral nature, only so far as they proceed from these internal affections. Human laws must be satisfied with external obedience, because human lawgivers cannot search the heart, nor scrutinize the motives of those who owe obedience. But even earthly judges, in administering justice, endeavour as far as human judgment can go, to discover from what internal motives any action under examination was performed; and their decision of acquittal or condemnation is grounded on the opinion which they form of the intention and motives of the person under arraignment. Much more then does the moral Governor of the World require of his creatures the obedience of the heart; for he possesses a perfect knowledge of what is in the heart of every one; and a most perfect estimate of the nature of moral good and evil as those qualities exist in the human heart. It seems evident, therefore, that the laws of nature demand the highest degree of excellence of which the mind of man is capable. And as God possesses every moral attribute in the highest perfection, it is reasonable to infer, that man, as he came from the hands of his Creator, was endued with the seeds and principles of every moral virtue. And if the nature of man is not now found adorned with these moral excellencies, he must in the exercise of his free will have departed from his primeval state. Our present inquiry, however, is not whether man has fallen from his original integrity, but what are the duties arising out of man's relation to God as his Creator, Benefactor, and Preserver. Although

Infinite excellency.

the obligation to obedience arises primarily from the relations just mentioned, yet it is necessary to take into view the supreme excellence and majesty of the character of God; for if pious and devout sentiments towards God be required, it is because there is in the character of God as exhibited in his works, something to call forth such affections, from rational and rightly disposed minds. If God were not supremely excellent, it would not be reasonable to demand supreme love from his creatures, and so of other things. But as we know that God is possessed of every excellence in an infinite degree, there exists an object for every affection and sentiment toward him, of which the human mind is capable. From what has been said it is evident, that in order to perform any other duties to the Creator, some knowledge of his true character is requisite. Without knowledge the rational mind cannot exercise right affections.

Adoration

Supposing then a rational mind, such as it is reasonable to think man possessed, when he proceeded from the hands of his Maker, and possessing that knowledge of his attributes which may be learned from his works, what would be the first thoughts and feelings of the newly created soul? In our judgment, the first feeling would be an emotion of profound veneration, or perhaps the word *adoration* would more strongly indicate the state of the mind, absorbed in the contemplation of a Being so august, so powerful, and so immense. This feeling, then, is one which ought to exist in every rational mind toward the Almighty. This is the true foundation of divine worship. It is the deep and solemn emotion which is the essence of the worship, which holy beings in all worlds offer unto God.

Reverence.

And this feeling would lead to a reverence of every thing which has any relation to God. His very name would be sacred. We have read of men of great eminence who never mentioned that name without a solemn pause, or some external token of reverence.

Thankfulness.

The duty which most naturally arises from the relation which man sustains to God, as his Creator, Benefactor, and Redeemer, is that of gratitude. This is when strong a very lively and impulsive feeling. It draws men along as taken captive; and yet the constraint is not painful, but pleasing. Under the influence of gratitude, men will engage in the most odious duties, and will voluntarily make the most self-denying sacrifices. Under the influence of this affection men have been willing to lay down their lives. Gratitude is then an important principle of man's obedience. It is true, some have attempted to degrade this principle as one which scarcely can be said to partake of the nature of virtue, because it has respect to self, and to our own interest. But though gratitude originates in the sense of benefits received by ourselves, it deserves not to be classed with mere selfish affections. Its object is to make a return to a benefactor for favour received. It is, therefore, an elevated species of justice; for when a suitable and adequate return can be made for favours received, gratitude will not be satisfied until this s done. And in regard to the benefits received from our Creator, as an adequate compensation is utterly beyond our power, gratitude manifests itself in acknowledgment of obligation in thanksgiving and in unceasing praises. There is, however, no necessity to argue this matter; the ap peal may safely be made to the feelings of every rightly constituted mind. All men who acknowledge the existence and Providence of God, feel that a debt of gratitude is due to their great Benefactor.

Love.

As the mind, when uncorrupted, is so constituted as to love and esteem whatever is excellent, and as moral excellence is superior to all other amiable objects; and as God possesses this excellence in an infinite degree, it is reasonable that he should be esteemed above every other object. Finite minds, it is true, can never exercise love proportionate to the excellence of this Glorious Being; but as far as they possess the capacity of apprehending it, and the susceptibility of affection, they are under moral obligation to love God with all their powers. And this cannot be considered as demanding too much of the rational creature, for no other measure of affection can be fixed without supposing a wrong estimate of the object, or a defect of right feeling; for what is more reasonable than to proportion the intensity of our affection to the excellence of the object? But in this also, the excellency of the object infinitely surpasses our capacity of love, so that if the mind should be enlarged a thousand-fold, so as to possess a thousand times as great a power of love and esteem as at present, the obligation to love God with this increasing capacity would be complete; and any less degree of esteem and care would be casting dishonour on God. And again, this obligation would exist, even if it were painful to come up in our affections to this high demand; but this is so far from being the fact, that man's happiness is perfect in the same proportion as his obedience is perfect. From every consideration, therefore, it is evident that man is bound by the law of his nature, and the relation which he sustains to God, to love him with his whole soul.

Submission.

As the will of God is always guided by wisdom and goodness, whenever and however this will is manifested, it should be implicitly and cheerfully submitted to, even though contrary to our wishes, and even what seems best to our reason; which is submission to the Providence of God.

Another duty clearly incumbent on the rational creature of God, is trust or confidence.

Trust. As man is dependent, and as the supply of his necessities can be derived from no other source than from God, it is evidently his duty to place his confidence in God for every thing, believing in his goodness, faithfulness and power.

This trust in God, however, involves the duty of prayer. It is as natural and reasonable

Prayer. for a dependent creature to apply to its Creator for what it needs, as for a child thus to solicit the aid of a parent who is believed to have the disposition and ability to bestow what it needs. Plausible objections have been raised against the duty of prayer, derived from the omniscience of God, and from his immutable purposes. But these objections possess no real validity. For although God knows perfectly beforehand what his creatures need, yet the acknowledgment of their dependence is manifestly proper, and the offering of petitions for such things as they need, has a tendency to keep up a proper sense of dependence. And as God deals with his creatures according to the nature which he has given them, it is proper that he should require of them such dispositions and acts as are becoming independent creatures. This, too, is in accordance with the conduct of men on whom others are dependent. The object of prayer, including praise, is to preserve in the mind a right state of feeling towards a Being to whom it owes every thing, and from whom alone blessings can be expected. The highest privilege of the most exalted creature is to enjoy communion and intercourse with the Infinite Source of all good. Prayer is the only means which man enjoys of holding immediate intercourse with his Maker. And this privilege is the highest honour which he can enjoy in the present state. So also, it is a means of the most sublime happiness. By this exercise he draws near to God, and when such approaches are made sincerely and affectionately on his part, it cannot be doubted that Divine communications will be vouchsafed, and the light of the Divine favour be lifted upon him, and the answer to his prayers be granted by the dispensations of divine Providence toward him.

Not inconsistent with Divine plan.

As to the objection derived from the immutability of the Divine purposes, it arises from a narrow view of this subject, which leaves out an important part of the Divine plan. The purposes of God, though immutable, are not inconsistent with the freedom of the creatures, nor with the use and efficacy of appropriate means. The truth is, all these acts and means are included in the Divine plan. If God has decreed that a certain field shall produce a plentiful crop; he has also decreed that all the influences of sun, rain, and the necessary labour shall take place. And if he has purposed to bestow certain favours on his rational creatures, he may in the same manner purpose that these benefits shall be given in answer to prayer; so that prayer may be considered as the means by which these blessings are obtained as truly as a plentiful crop is the effect of a skilful and laborious tillage of the ground.

As to external acts of devotion, reason and

nature teach that humility and reverence in our words, attitudes, and gestures are highly proper when we address our praises unto God. When we are filled with devotional feelings, nature prompts to give utterance to our emotions; and the use of appropriate sounds and gestures seems also to keep up and increase the feelings of the mind. These outward expressions, however, are not essential to acceptable prayer. The silent breathings of desire are known to God, and will be acceptable to him. It is reasonable to believe that God never takes more complacency in his creatures, than when they come before him in the humble, reverential posture of adoration, prayer, and praise.

Outward acts of religion.

Nothing can be more evident, than that the creature should exercise benevolence or good will towards the Author of his being. Not that we can desire Him to be more excellent, more wise, more powerful, or more independent than he is; but we may rejoice in all his attributes and glory in his greatness, and be delighted with the idea

Reference to the glory of God.

of his unbounded and uninterrupted happiness; and in these elevated emotions of joy, and acts of glorying and glorifying God, it is believed that the purest, sublimest, and most constant happiness of all holy beings consists. Nothing is more evident to impartial reason, than that the glory of God should be the supreme object of the rational creature's pursuit. It is, in fact, the noblest object which can be considered. We are unable to imagine any thing more glorious for God himself to seek, than his own glory. Certainly, then, it is the highest end at which any creature can aim; and it is a sentiment entirely accordant with reason, that all the creation was produced for the purpose of exhibiting the glory of God. And man was endowed with a capacity of knowing and loving God, for the very purpose of glorifying his Maker. Not that any addition can be made to the essential perfection and felicity of the Eternal One; but the manifestation of these perfections is what is properly called the glory of God.

All the duties which have been specified,

commend themselves, as obligatory on the rational creature, to every impartial mind; all that seems further necessary is to give a brief summary of what has been said on this subject. Summary.

The order in which these devotional exercises are set down is not very important; for though there is an order of precedence and sequence in all our mental exercises, yet while it is unnecessary to speak of these affections which have God for their object, seriatim, they are commonly combined and mingled in the conscious experience of the mind; so that in the same moment various acts and exercises appear to be simultaneous. They may, however, be all comprehended under the single term, *Love*, if we give a genuine meaning to that term. All included in love.

The summation which seems as proper as any other which occurs, is the following:

1. *Adoration*, having for its object the greatness, majesty, holiness, and incomprehensibility of God. Duties to God.

2. *Admiration*, or holy wonder of the wis-

dom of God in the multiplied contrivances and organizations in the created universe.

3. *Esteem for and complacency in God's moral excellence.*

4. *Desire of Union and Communion with God*, and of conformity to his character.

5. *Gratitude* for his goodness manifested in all creation; but particularly to man, in the constitution of his soul and body, and in the provision made by the providence of God for the subsistence and comfort of the human family, and of all living creatures.

6. *Trust, or Confidence in God*, as a benignant and kind Father and Protector, who will not abandon the work of his own hands, nor be wanting in contributing to their happiness in future, as long as they are obedient to his will.

7. *Acquiescence in the will of God*, and submission to those dispensations which even cross the natural feelings, is an evident moral duty. Indeed, the surrender of soul and body to God, to be used and disposed of by him for his own glory, is the state of mind of which the moral faculty approves.

8. *Prayer to God* for such things as we need, is a duty dictated by the law of nature, including suitable expressions of our devotional feelings in words and gestures. But no creature has a right to institute or adopt any ceremonies of worship which God has not appointed.

9. *Making the Glory of God the supreme end of all his actions*, the object of his constant and untiring pursuit; and rejoicing and triumphing in the infinite glory, independence, immutability, and blessedness of God.

The above enumeration, it is believed, comprehends the internal acts and exercises in which the duty of man to God consists, which duties plainly arise out of the attributes of God and man's relation to him, as his Creator, Preserver, and Benefactor. And if man had never failed in the performance of these duties—if he had continued to exercise those affections which spontaneously spring up in his soul, when he came from the hands of his Creator, this world, instead of being a land of misery, would now have been a blooming paradise of joy. And we may be sure that

What reason af firms of man's fall en state.

a good God who loves all his creatures according to their actions, would never have permitted the natural evils which now oppress the human soul, to have entered into the world. Sickness, famine, and death in its thousand different forms, would have been unknown.

Conclusion.

It is evident from the slightest view of the character of man in all ages and countries, that he has lost his primeval integrity, that the whole race have by some means fallen into the dark gulf of sin and misery. This, reason teaches; but how to escape from this wretched condition, she teaches not.

FINIS.

CPSIA information can be obtained
at www.ICGtesting.com
Printed in the USA
LVHW110813120522
718525LV00003B/83

9 783375 001476